'You don't g shining arm knight in dus

Again he held out me, Katie? Don't you remember...?'

Kate felt embarrassment start way down in her toes and wash upward through her body.

'Grant? Grant Bell?' Her voice was so faint it was a wonder he heard it.

'Aha, you do remember!' he said, and she had a feeling his delight stemmed more from the hectic colour in her cheeks than from her muttered delivery of his name.

'So! Shall I come in?'

'No!'

Kate wasn't sure why she'd said it so firmly, but Grant Bell had been trouble all his life, and there was no way she was inviting him into her house. Particularly now, when she had the baby to consider.

And even more particularly now, when bits of her she'd thought would lie dormant for ever were reacting, if not to his presence then to the almost forgotten memories he'd conjured up.

Meredith Webber was previously a teacher, shop-keeper, travel agent, pig farmer, builder and worker in the disability field (among other things). She says, 'The "writing bug" struck me unexpectedly. I entered a competition run by a women's magazine, shared the third prize with two hundred and fifty other would-be writers, and found myself infected. Thirty-something books later, I'm still suffering. Medical romances appeal to me because they offer the opportunity to include a wider cast of characters, and the challenge of interweaving a love story into the drama of medical or paramedical practice.'

Recent titles by the same author:

THE MARRIAGE GAMBLE
A WOMAN WORTH WAITING FOR
HER DR WRIGHT
THE TEMPTATION TEST
A VERY PRECIOUS GIFT
REDEEMING DR HAMMOND

CHRISTMAS KNIGHT

BY
MEREDITH WEBBER

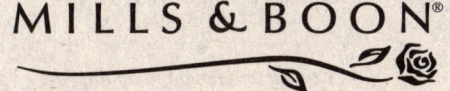

DID YOU PURCHASE THIS BOOK WITHOUT A COVER?

If you did, you should be aware it is **stolen property** as it was reported *unsold and destroyed* by a retailer. Neither the author nor the publisher has received any payment for this book.

All the characters in this book have no existence outside the imagination of the author, and have no relation whatsoever to anyone bearing the same name or names. They are not even distantly inspired by any individual known or unknown to the author, and all the incidents are pure invention.

All Rights Reserved including the right of reproduction in whole or in part in any form. This edition is published by arrangement with Harlequin Enterprises II B.V. The text of this publication or any part thereof may not be reproduced or transmitted in any form or by any means, electronic or mechanical, including photocopying, recording, storage in an information retrieval system, or otherwise, without the written permission of the publisher.

This book is sold subject to the condition that it shall not, by way of trade or otherwise, be lent, resold, hired out or otherwise circulated without the prior consent of the publisher in any form of binding or cover other than that in which it is published and without a similar condition including this condition being imposed on the subsequent purchaser.

MILLS & BOON and MILLS & BOON with the Rose Device are registered trademarks of the publisher.

First published in Great Britain 2002
Harlequin Mills & Boon Limited,
Eton House, 18-24 Paradise Road, Richmond, Surrey TW9 1SR

© Meredith Webber 2002

ISBN 0 263 83100 0

Set in Times Roman 10½ on 11¼ pt.
03-1102-53696

Printed and bound in Spain
by Litografia Rosés, S.A., Barcelona

CHAPTER ONE

TROUBLE rode into Testament on a hot sultry summer afternoon. The storm clouds hanging low above the lone motorcycle rider were nearly as black as the full suit of leathers he wore.

The shiny black and chrome bike tooled slowly up the main street, then turned and came back down.

'Here's trouble,' Mrs Ellis, on the stoop outside the newsagent's, said to no one in particular.

'Trouble if there's more than one of them,' Dick Harris, the local police sergeant, muttered to his constable.

'Trouble looking for somewhere to stop!' old man Carey, who was propping up the table by the window of the pub, told his mate Digger, though Digger showed little interest, continuing to sniff at a greasy spot on the pub floor as if it might offer a new taste sensation.

The bike slowed outside the pub, and a helmeted head turned towards the building, as if the rider might be tempted to try a cold one, then the motor revved, and the rider continued. Down the street, past the school, then left towards the northern end of town.

Another tourist passing through.

Those inhabitants of Testament who'd seen him pass forgot about him, though perhaps with an unidentified sense of regret, as if a little excitement might have brightened up their lives.

In the big house next door to the hospital, Kate Fenton knew nothing of this. She was in her bedroom, peering down into a crib and giving the little alien who'd so disrupted her life what for!

'The trouble with you is,' she said, to the now sleeping

baby, 'you've got no sense of timing. No understanding of the simple words, Wait just a minute. If we could sort this out, we might get somewhere, but, no, you're just like your father—demanding instant gratification.'

She heard her own words, cursed loudly, then added apologetically, 'I'm sorry for that last remark. I swore I'd never use that "just like your father" phrase. After all, I'm the one who decided to have you, so I can hardly blame him for anything, can I? Particularly not when he's washed his hands of both of us.'

The baby moved milk-rimmed lips and slept on, while Kate studied the tiny face, the dark eyelashes like feathery caterpillars against the still crumpled skin, the miniature fingers clenched into fists as if the little scrap was ready to take on the world.

'Damn, but you're useless!' she muttered, swearing for the second time in as many minutes. If she didn't stop this habit right now, the 'damn' word would be the first the baby said.

And that thought made her say it again, though she did promise herself it would be the last—the very last—time! 'Jeez Louise', her favourite expression of despair back when she was a student, still living at home, might work. Though it would mean dicing Louise from the 'perhapses' for a name.

A rumbling outside made her glance towards the French doors, open to catch the slightest hint of breeze. The storm must be closer than she'd thought. Though the next sound, footsteps across the front veranda followed by a pounding on the front door, suggested the rumbling noise might have been something else.

She cast one final and now worried glance at the baby, then walked, soft-footed, to the bedroom door, closing it behind her. Her stomach cramped with the anxiety that had been such a totally unexpected consequence of giving birth, she doubted she'd ever get used to it.

Given the heat, the front door was also wide open, so, as she stepped into the hall, she saw the tall, dark-clad figure looming in the square of light, and beyond it, on the drive, a hulking black and silver monster of a motorbike. Her anxiety turned to panic.

'Can I help you?' she said, moving quickly as if speed might somehow lessen any risk to the baby.

'Dr Fenton?'

There was so much doubt and disbelief in the deep male voice that Kate found herself checking her body to make sure she was dressed. These days, if there'd been no morning surgery, she was just as likely to be in her night-attire at midday.

But today she was OK—her post-pregnancy tummy squashed into old jeans, and a reasonably milk-free cropped top ending somewhere near her midriff.

'Yes,' she said, stepping more cautiously towards him now.

'Katie Fenton, the bank manager's daughter?'

The 'd' word reverberated in her head again, but she managed to keep it internal, while peering at the leather-clad colossus leaning negligently on her doorjamb.

Was she supposed to know him? Was it someone with whom she'd been at school?

'You're supposed to be pregnant!' he said, in such accusing tones she almost apologised, but by now she could see his face more clearly, and a vague stirring of memory, more sensory than mental, was shifting her emotions to a new level of disquiet.

'Pregnancies aren't permanent, you know,' she told him, telling herself it couldn't possibly be Grant Bell. The Bells had all left town when the bank had foreclosed on their property—her father's bank, in fact. She herself had heard Grant say no one would ever see him in Testament again—words which, at the time, had broken her heart...

'You mean you've already had the baby? When? Where

is it? You *did* keep it, I assume. And how the hell have you been handling the practice, childbirth and a new baby all on your own?'

He sounded cross, but not nearly as cross as she was becoming, standing here in her own hall, being berated by a stranger—whether he was Grant Bell or not.

'With a great deal of difficulty, if you must know,' she told him, hoping the ice she'd managed to inject into her voice might stop him asking personal questions. 'Now, if you want to see me professionally, the surgery, which is through the side entrance to the yard, will open at six.' Then she remembered it was Sunday. 'No, it won't, but you can go to the hospital and if they need me they'll call.'

She moved forward, intending to shut the door, then realised he was leaning against the hinged side of it.

He must have guessed her intentions for he stepped backwards, but put up a hand.

'It's too darned hot to shut it. Anyway, I'm coming in.'

He began to strip off his leather jacket as he spoke, peeling it away like a second skin, to reveal a lurid Hawaiian shirt, printed with unlikely flowers in shades of red, green and purple. Then, as the leather jacket was slung on a chair near the door, he started on the trousers, unzipping them, then easing them down over blue board shorts and long, solid legs with a sheen of dark hair slicked to them by the leather.

Kate dragged her eyes away from the legs for long enough to recall his final sentence.

'There's no surgery today but the hospital is just next door,' she repeated, because 'no, you can't come in' would have sounded rude to a stranger. Certainly to a stranger bigger and stronger than she was.

He glanced up from reefing his boots off his feet, and as he grinned at her, she realised it might, indeed, be Grant Bell.

'I've not come as a patient, but as your knight in shining

armour.' He straightened and spread his arms wide as if presenting himself for inspection. 'Do you still read fantasy romances, Katie Fenton?'

'Kate, not Katie,' she said in her most professional tones, then she realised her name wasn't the point—his was! 'Who *are* you?'

Her visitor grinned, his blue eyes gleaming in his suntanned face.

'You don't go for the knight in shining armour? How about a knight in dusty leathers?' Again he held out his arms. 'Don't you know me, Katie? Don't you remember the boy who—?'

Kate felt embarrassment start way down in her toes and wash upward through her body, so her thighs and breasts and cheeks all burned with it.

'Grant? Grant Bell?' Her voice was so faint—forget the voice, *she* was so faint—it was a wonder he heard it.

'Aha, you do remember!' he said, and she had a feeling his delight stemmed more from the hectic colour in her cheeks than from her muttered delivery of his name.

'So! Shall I come in?'

'No!'

Kate wasn't sure why she'd said it so firmly, but Grant Bell had been trouble all his life, and there was no way she was inviting him into her house. Particularly now, when she had the baby to consider.

And more particularly now, when bits of her she'd thought would lie dormant for ever were reacting, if not to his presence then to the almost forgotten memories he'd conjured up.

'No!' she said again, frowning at him to reinforce the word, while he was studying her, if not with a frown then with a definitely puzzled look in his eyes.

'But—' he began.

'No!' she said again, then, right on cue, a thin wail rose above the distant rumble—this time it *was* thunder—and

Kate knew it was only a matter of seconds before the wail became a demand and, seconds past that stage, a furious complaint.

'The baby's crying.' Grant stated the obvious while Kate hesitated, wanting to shut the door, to shut him out, but knowing every other door onto the veranda was open so shutting this one was no guarantee of keeping him out. 'How old is it? Was it premmie, or did you have your dates wrong?'

He grinned as he asked the last question, and once again hot flushes of embarrassment flooded her body, as more memories returned to mortify her.

'I've got to go,' she gabbled at him, and now she did shut the door.

As the noise had reached demand stage, she went straight to the bedroom, lifted the red-faced mite from the bassinet and held the tiny form against her shoulder, patting her gently on the back and murmuring soothing nothings to her.

The baby obliged by burping sickly-sweet-smelling milk onto Kate's shoulder, so she felt the dampness seep through her cotton top to her skin—skin which was still hot with memories of Grant Bell, explaining the facts of life to her, though using cattle as examples so her knowledge of sex, at twelve, was badly skewed.

A mistake not sorted out in spite of sex education classes, until she was sixteen, when he'd demonstrated how it worked with humans, down by the creek, one hot and humid summer afternoon, two days before her father had foreclosed on Grant's parents' property and a month before the family had left the district for ever.

'Didn't you know I was coming? Didn't Aunt Vi tell you?'

The cause of her embarrassment walked through the French doors.

'The baby looks as if it's gone back to sleep. Is it a girl or a boy? What did you call it?'

He'd never waited for an answer to his questions, Kate remembered, as she set aside the last series to concentrate on the first.

'Tell me what?' she demanded. 'What was Vi supposed to tell me?'

Once again, Grant spread his arms wide.

'That I was coming,' he said, so obviously pleased with himself Kate wanted to throw something.

But all she had to hand was the baby, so that wasn't a good idea.

She settled the little one back into the bassinet, then, knowing for sure that Grant Bell on her veranda was better than Grant Bell in her house, she walked towards him, put one hand on his chest and pushed him back out the door.

Well, she pushed and he backed up. Had he not wanted to move she doubted whether he'd have gone anywhere.

'What's with you?' he complained, grasping her by the shoulders to stop her pushing him any further. 'Why the antagonism? If anyone should be feeling leftover anger, it's me, Angel-Face. After all, it was your father who tossed my family off the property.'

'It was the bank that foreclosed. My father was just the instrument they used. He hated doing it,' Kate told him, then she added, a little late and with far too little venom, 'And don't call me Angel-Face.'

Broad shoulders lifted in a shrug and a cheeky smile that had, if anything, improved with the years stretched his lips.

'Sorry, Katie,' he said softly, and she had to step away from him before she could reply.

'And don't call me that either! Katie's a kid's name and, in case you hadn't noticed, I'm all grown up now.'

Eyes as blue as summer skies skimmed across her body, scorching where they touched.

'Oh, I'd noticed,' he murmured, and the way he said it made her conscious of her untoned stomach, overly large breasts and the damp, smelly milk stain. 'So, what do I call you? Katherine? Dr Fenton?'

'You don't have to call me anything, because you won't be seeing any more of me. It would have been great to catch up, and I hope you enjoy your visit to Vi, but right now I'm flat out, what with the baby and the practice and all, so we might as well say goodbye and you can get on your bike and ride off into the sunset.'

It was a pretty good speech, she thought, then her brain, which hadn't been working well for months and seemed to have lost even more usable cells since she'd given birth, prompted her to add, 'My friends call me Kate.'

His smile finally faded, which made looking at him slightly easier, though now she could see past its attraction to the little lines fanned out from his eyes, the faint furrows in his forehead, the fine creases that smile had pressed into his cheeks.

Grant Bell—all grown up!

All grown up into a ruggedly handsome man.

'Katie,' he said, speaking slowly as if he realised her brain cells were dying by the million, 'I'm here to stay. I'm your locum. Didn't Vi explain? The woman who was to come took up a permanent position, and the agency was scrabbling to find someone. Vi knew I was at a loose end for a couple of months, so she got in touch and here I am.'

He did the hands-outstretched thing again, as if offering himself to her as the answer not only to her problems but to all the troubles of the universe. Just so had he held his arms when, as a sexy, hormonally charged teenager, he'd offered himself to most of the girls in high school. Back then the gesture had meant 'Hey, take me, I'm yours.' And most of them probably had!

Right now, Kate didn't know what it meant, though she did know she shouldn't even think about it.

Grant Bell was trouble. He'd been trouble back then, and he was still trouble now. Just the way her body warmed to his gaze, and reacted to his grin, told her that. And now she was a mother, with an infant daughter to consider, someone like Grant Bell gave a whole new dimension to the 't' word.

She frowned at him, set aside, with difficulty, the 'trouble' thing and considered the words that had accompanied his gesture.

'You're here because my locum couldn't make it?' she said. She'd obviously lost far more brain cells than she'd realised. 'But I need a doctor, not a—' her eyes took in the lurid shirt and board shorts '—beach bum!'

He managed to look hurt, but he'd been able to do that since she'd first met him when he'd pulled one of her ringletty curls in church, then had denied being the culprit when she'd turned to glare at him.

'Beach bum?' he echoed, with such incredulity it *had* to be false. 'I'll have you know I was on holiday when Aunt Vi's summons came, and I left the waves at Byron Bay to come racing to your rescue.' He grinned again. 'The knight thing, you know.'

'I think I'd better sit down,' Kate muttered, while telling herself giving birth couldn't possibly have killed *all* her brain cells.

Ever the gentleman, Grant used his foot to hook a chair towards her, then, as she sank gratefully into it, he propped himself against the railing, folded his arms and gave the impression of a man willing to wait for ever, if she needed that long.

But wait for what?

The locum who wasn't coming?

An explanation of why Vi had contacted Grant and, more to the point, why he'd come?

Kate stared up at him, hoping the horror dawning in her mind wasn't visible on her face.

'Did you— No, you couldn't have— Surely not—'

'Are you going to finish any of those questions or is it

a new guessing game that hasn't reached the wilds of Byron Bay?' he asked.

'Why are you here?' she asked, though reasonably sure she'd asked it before and the answer hadn't helped.

Grant did the arms-outstretched thing again and she managed, with difficulty, not to think about sex.

'I'm your locum.'

'You're a doctor?'

On a scale of one to ten, her disbelief would have ricocheted off the chart at about one hundred and seventy-five.

'Y-you can't b-be!' she stuttered, answering her own demand because he was doing the hurt look again. 'You were always more interested in animals than people. Why be a doctor?'

'Well, there was a time when you were going to be a missionary and save the heathen, until I pointed out to you that most of the so-called heathen had perfectly good religions of their own and wouldn't want you.' He grinned, again, and added, 'And as you're obviously not a missionary, why shouldn't I be a doctor?'

Kate couldn't find an answer to that question. He'd been bright enough, though his extra-curricular activities of chasing either cattle or girls had meant his high school grades had never been excellent.

But the question of whether or not he was a doctor wasn't the issue—him being here was. She'd intended for her locum to live in—the house was certainly big enough for two people and a very small, almost minute baby—but having Grant Bell move in was asking for—well, the only word for it, though certainly not strong enough, was trouble.

She had to say no—to stop this before it went any further.

'I wanted a woman—Vi knew that. I put flowered sheets on the bed.'

Even before she'd finished speaking she knew it had been the wrong thing to say.

Grant didn't smile but she suspected laughter was lurking in his eyes when he said, very gently, 'I don't see flowered sheets as an assault on my masculinity.'

'But we'll be sharing the house,' Kate protested.

'Worried about what people will think?'

She looked blankly at him.

'If I was worried about what people think, I wouldn't have come back here single and pregnant,' she snapped. 'I'm worried—'

She stopped dead. Telling Grant Bell the truth—that she was bothered by the thought he'd see her, tired, rumpled, milk-smelling and at her most unattractive as she ambled round the house in the early hours of the morning, grouching and grumbling as she tried to get with it enough to organise her day—just wasn't an option.

'You're worried?' he prompted.

'About sharing the house—sharing the kitchen and the bathroom. These old houses only ever had one, you know, and the baby cries, you'll be disturbed.'

'More disturbed than a woman by a baby crying? What happened to sexual equality? Or doesn't it apply to crying babies?'

The storm rumbled closer and a loud clap of thunder, followed by a vivid flash of jagged lightning, sent Kate scurrying back to the bedroom, certain the baby would be woken.

'Storms always come from the west, so I'll shut the doors on that side of the veranda,' Grant called after her.

Perhaps if he showed how useful he was it would make up for him not being a woman.

Though she *was* worried. He had seen it in the stiff set of her shoulders, the way her arms had wrapped protectively around her body, but her concern only made him more determined to stay—to help Katie Fenton, who, according to Aunt Vi, needed quite a bit of support right now.

He followed the veranda around to the front of the house and went into the hall, turning first into the lounge room to shut the two sets of French doors in there, then the dining room, thinking all the while of Katie.

He'd looked into her huge green eyes with the dusty gold lashes and seen the strain repeated there. Was it he who bothered her, or would any man have generated the same response?

And why?

Because whoever had fathered the baby had let her down?

That must be it. The bastard had turned her off men for good.

So if he neutralised himself in some way...

'What about your bike?' Kate called, and he cursed as he dashed back outside through raindrops as big as peanuts. Seeing Katie Fenton again must have rattled him more than he'd thought it would, as he'd forgotten to put the bike away.

He wheeled it into the garage where it fitted nicely beside the dark green Subaru she must drive.

A sensible, neutral kind of car, saying nothing much about the owner.

Neutral!

Neutralise. Perhaps he could do something to minimise whatever danger he represented to her.

He could pretend he was gay, but suspected Katie wouldn't fall for a sudden change in his sexual persuasion.

Still thinking, he grabbed his bags out of the luggage compartments and dashed back through the now thundering rain to the house. His shirt was sodden, clinging to him like an—

Over-friendly woman!

That was the answer. He might be a man, but a man attached to a woman was safe—neutralised!

He walked through to the kitchen, knowing from the rattling noises out there he'd find Katie—Kate.

'I must phone Chlorinda,' he said. 'Getting this lovely shirt wet reminded me.'

'Chlorinda!' Kate repeated, in such disbelieving tones he knew he'd made a huge mistake, but for reasons beyond his understanding the name had just popped out.

'My fiancée,' he explained.

The disbelief in her voice was equally apparent in Katie's beautiful eyes.

'No one's called Chlorinda these days,' she snorted, and, anxious to retrieve the situation, he tried again.

'Actually—' big shame-faced grin '—her name's Linda, but I can't help playing with names and somehow Linda, Chlorinda, you know how it happens. Like K-K-K-Katie, swallowed the ha'penny. Remember?'

'Of course I remember! You teased me with that stupid rhyme often enough.'

Fierce eyes flashed green fire, but he guessed the neutralising thing had worked.

He held up his bags.

'The bedroom? Where have you put me—or put the flowered sheets?'

She didn't answer, and the distracted way she pushed at her hair, at the heavy, dark blonde mass of riotous curls, suggested Vi had been right. Katie Fenton was just about at the end of her tether.

'You could stay with Vi,' she said, but there was no force in the suggestion, and before he'd had time to object she contradicted herself. 'But that's stupid. I wanted the locum here so I didn't have to change the phone around—so she could take the night and weekend calls.'

She glared at Grant.

'It's not a full-time position—you know that, don't you?

The woman who was coming was studying for another degree so didn't mind it being part time, job-sharing. Although there should be two doctors here. I tried to get the Health Department to agree to pay some of the locum's wages so it would be full time but that wretched Paul Newberry hasn't resigned. Apparently he's on stress leave…'

The distraction—almost panic—was in her voice now as well, and Grant found it hurt him to see Katie Fenton, who'd always been willing to take on the world—and any stupid dare her schoolmates had ever dreamed up—so uncertain.

'Look, why don't we sit down and have a cup of tea? In fact, you sit and I'll make it. It will show you how useful I am, and anyway, you've probably been doing far too much straight after the birth of the baby.'

She gave a funny little smile that held a hint of the Katie he remembered.

'Didn't you once tell me that in some countries women gave birth in the fields, wrapped the baby in a sling across their backs and kept working? I've been reminding myself of those stoical souls for the last ten days!'

'I was probably exaggerating—or the book I read it in wasn't telling the entire truth. And anyway, that's not you, so sit. I'll find the tea—or would you prefer coffee—no, you shouldn't have coffee, we don't want the baby addicted to caffeine from birth, now, do we?'

'Ten minutes in the house and already you're giving orders?' Kate said, but she sank down into the chair, certain she'd be better able to handle the situation while seated. She'd been tempted to say she wanted coffee, but she'd managed to wean herself of the caffeine habit while pregnant, and now, while the smell of coffee still pleased her, drinking it made her feel queasy.

She sank lower in the chair, and watched Grant Bell opening and shutting cupboard doors, the situation so bizarre it was easier to believe she was dreaming. In fact, she was tired enough for it to be a dream.

Then, because watching him was disturbing in ways she couldn't begin to understand, and bringing back not only the happy memories but the anguish she'd felt when he and his family had left town so many years ago, she leaned forward, folded her arms on the table and rested her head on them.

Just for a moment, she told herself, as her eyes slid shut.

Surprised to find she'd given in so easily, Grant turned to ask about milk and sugar, and found his companion sound asleep.

She *must* be exhausted, he thought, while the mix of pity and anger he felt made him wonder if the 'knight in shining armour' concept was as good as it had seemed back on the beach at Byron Bay, where the waves had been practically non-existent and he'd been bored by the holiday that had barely begun.

But whatever he felt, it was obvious Aunt Vi had been right. Katie Fenton needed help.

And he'd been available.

He made himself a cup of tea, and found a couple of cracker biscuits he could eat with it. If she had cheese—

A thin wail stopped his explorations of the refrigerator, and, certain Katie would wake if the baby continued to cry, he shot through to the bedroom, hesitating momentarily before bending to lift the tiny form from the crib. He actually hadn't thought about the baby part when launching into his knight act, but now he was here he'd just have to cope. After all, it was just another anonymous baby, like the hundreds he'd handled at the hospital over the last year.

'I didn't even ask your name,' he said, holding it close against his chest. 'And now you're making my shirt even wetter. But I can fix that. I'll change you. Would that be nice?'

Talking, rocking, moving all the time, he looked around

the room. There was a pile of folded nappies on the dressing-table, and various boxes and bottles of lotions and potions squashed alongside them.

'I'll check out the system Katie's using as I undress you,' he said, placing the little one on the bed then unwrapping a loose cotton cover from around it. 'Do the blue flowers on your singlet mean you're a boy? We'll soon find out, won't we? Though you're not as new as I thought you must be!'

He touched the still red navel, surprised to find the remnants of the umbilical cord already gone, then undid the nappy, discovering the new arrival was a girl. The system obviously decreed a blue nappy liner inside the nappy. Well, that was easy—they were in the box.

'Little Katie!' he murmured, leaving the outer covering flat on the bed while he gave in to temptation and marvelled at the miniature limbs and digits—the tiny, perfect finger- and toenails. His heart tightened, memories crowding in, but he couldn't help but tell her, 'You're beautiful, did you know that? Does your mummy tell you all the time?'

He fastened the nappy with deft, remembered actions, found a clean cotton sheet and rewrapped his charge, but the idea that Katie Fenton was the mummy in question was causing him as much internal confusion as the baby.

'She was always trouble,' he told the infant as he returned her to the crib. 'I was always getting her out of it.'

He rocked the crib until the little eyelids dropped and dark lashes fanned out over rose-petal cheeks.

'Or getting her into it,' honesty forced him to add.

CHAPTER TWO

THE ringing noise startled Kate awake, but she'd been so deeply asleep it took a moment to realise where she was. Asleep at the kitchen table?

And dreaming of Grant Bell, of all people!

By the time she'd set the dream aside, wiped what felt suspiciously like drool from her cheek and stood up, the ringing had stopped, but there was another noise—more unusual, frightening even. A man's voice!

As she walked, slowly and cautiously, towards the living room she realised Grant Bell hadn't been a dream. He was here—right in front of her, now she was in the doorway—and apparently intending to stay.

Her locum!

'Yes, Mrs Barrett, it's great to be back. No, I haven't seen Vi yet, but if George's in pain, shouldn't we be talking about him?'

He paused and Kate imagined the torrent of words pouring through the receiver from Mrs Barrett.

'She'd talk under water,' Grant said, smiling happily at Kate as he hung up. 'George has had a back spasm. Has it happened since you've been here? Any advice or should I just go out there and help the poor chap onto his bed and order him to stay there until it gets better?'

'I haven't seen him as a patient since I've been here,' Kate said, then honesty forced her to continue, 'Haven't seen a lot of the older men. Going to a woman doctor is evidently a worse admission of weakness than going to one of the males of the species. If they were desperate, they went to the hospital to see Paul—when he was here!'

She'd barely finished speaking when another thought struck her.

'Actually, that's a good reason for me to go, rather than you. It's a great way to break the ice and maybe prove something to the man. The Barretts' place is Kintower, isn't it? Out on the western road. I'll get the baby.'

'Get the baby?' Grant's voice was charged with disbelief. 'I've just changed her and put her back to sleep and you're going to wake her and take her out there? In a storm?'

Damn— Jeez Louise! What the hell was she thinking?

If Grant hadn't been there, she'd have thumped her forehead with the heel of her hand.

'I'll call Tara to come over and watch the baby,' Kate muttered, moving determinedly towards the phone although her reluctance to leave Tara in charge when she was farther away than next door at the hospital made her head ache. She knew Tara was good, but the girl did tend to lose herself in whatever she was reading...

Though Grant was here...

Right here! Grabbing her shoulders, giving her a little shake.

'Get with it, Katie,' he said, almost roughly. 'You've got a locum so you don't have to go out on calls. The locum goes, and that's me. Now's not the time to be proving yourself to George Barrett or any of the other dinosaurs in town. Now's the time to be thinking of your own well-being, and if you can't manage that, at least put the baby first.'

He was so close Kate could see the dark shadow of beard beneath the tanned skin on his chin—see individual follicles, and the outline of his lips...

You have a baby and he has a fiancée, an inner voice reminded her.

'Though I will take your car, if that's OK. You've a bag in it?'

The lips were moving but the words weren't making

much sense as she struggled to come to terms with feelings that *had* to be a hangover from the past.

'Keys?'

Keys? Car keys, presumably.

'In the kitchen, hanging over the cupboard near the back door.' She answered automatically and he moved away. Then, as if released from a spell, her heartbeat settled and her mind began working again. She hurried after him.

'Have you had any experience as a GP? Are you qualified to be doing this?'

He turned and grinned at her.

'Rather late to be asking those questions, isn't it, Katie? What do you think? I'm really a criminal on the run and Aunt Vi is helping me hide with this locum thing? Actually, if you go into your spare bedroom and open the briefcase in there, you'll see a file with all my qualifications and experience in it.'

He lifted the keys from the hook, and repeated his question.

'You've a medical bag in the car?'

She nodded.

'In the back,' she said, and was about to add more when he smiled again.

'Of course, papers can be forged,' he reminded her, and dashed out into the rain.

I shouldn't have said that, Grant admitted to himself as he drove out along the once-familiar road to the Barretts' property. He was here to help her, not to make things worse. But Katie Fenton had always responded so well to his teasing that the impulse had been irresistible.

He peered ahead through the slashing rain, looking for the gateposts that marked the entrance to Kintower. For her to have even considered bringing the baby out in the storm showed how rattled she must be. No wonder Vi had sent the SOS.

But why had he answered the call? The question had

nagged at him on the five-hundred-kilometre ride northwest, and, though he had plenty of glib replies—the surf was poor, he was bored with holidaying, Katie had been a friend, seeing Testament again so he could finally shut the door on the past—none of them seemed particularly satisfactory.

Particularly not when you considered the baby as part of the equation—although when Vi had phoned, the baby had, supposedly, been many weeks from the due date.

Or Vi had deliberately not mentioned its arrival...

The gateposts appeared and he swung cautiously off the road, aware that the red soil shoulders turned to treacherously slippery slush with a bit of rain. Thank heavens the Barretts' drive was sealed. After the long ride, he was glad he didn't have to handle a slick mud surface, though the neat Subaru, with constant four-wheel-drive, should have performed OK.

Mrs Barrett was on her front veranda, waving to him as if he might, by some mischance, miss the house. It was the only visible building though he knew there were sheds behind the grove of trees at the back of the house. He leaned over to grab the bag, noting with approval the properly secured capsule harness in the back seat, then dashed through the rain to the Barretts' front veranda.

'He's in the tractor shed. I left him there. He called me a stupid woman and pushed me away, so I left him there.'

Mrs Barrett seemed quite pleased by this decision, but Grant, soaked to the skin again, felt she could have told him this on the phone, or at least pointed to the area behind the house, rather than waving.

He refused her—surely inappropriate—offer of a cup of tea and raced back to the car. Backed up, and turned towards the sheds, pleased, as he approached, to see space where he could drive in and so save himself another wetting.

George Barrett was at one end, his body dwarfed by a

huge tractor. He was bent over, as if peering at the wheel studs, but Grant guessed from his pale complexion he was that way because any alternative was sheer agony.

Grant walked towards him, reading surprise and something like relief in the man's face.

'I don't know who you are,' George said, 'but can you give me a hand? There's a camp bed in the room out the back. If you can get me onto it, I can stay there until the damned thing stops paining.'

The thundering rain on the roof meant he'd had to shout to be heard.

'I can do better than that,' Grant shouted back, pulling the bag out of the back of the vehicle. 'I'm Grant Bell, Doug's son. I ended up studying medicine and I'm here helping Dr Fenton for a few weeks.'

He reached George's side, and rested his hand on the man's shoulder.

'Bad, is it?'

'Too right it's bad!' George muttered, the words almost inaudible given the background noise. 'Think I'd be here counting the cracks in the tractor tyre if it weren't?'

'How's the rest of your health? Any other problems? Allergies? Kidneys OK? Are you on any regular medication for your heart, blood pressure, arthritis?'

He raised his voice loudly enough to be heard, and at the same time opened the bag and searched through the neatly maintained compartments until he found the vial he wanted.

'Could we discuss this when I'm lying down?' George demanded, and Grant hid a grin.

'As long as I know you're not going to keel over on me from a drug interaction, I can give you a shot of morphine that will make getting from where you are to a bed a whole lot easier.'

He drew the liquid into the syringe and set it aside while he found a sterile swab.

'I don't take anything,' George finally admitted. 'I'm supposed to take things for my back but they don't make a scrap of difference, so why bother?'

'Have you had spasms like this before?' Grant asked, pushing up the man's sleeve and swabbing the skin above the biceps.

'No! It gets crook from time to time, and then I take the tablets and when it gets better I stop.'

'Fair enough,' Grant told him. 'Now, here goes. Hang on a bit and it should ease.'

He slid the needle into the muscle and injected the fluid. Relief wouldn't be instantaneous, but before long he should be able to help George to the bed. He filled the waiting time by cautiously examining his patient, but very little could be felt, and George's assertion that all he'd done had been to bend over to check the tyre pressure on the tractor tyre suggested a muscle spasm probably associated with deterioration in the spine.

The rain was still rattling down on the tin roof above them, so putting George to bed for a week in the shed wasn't all that good an option.

'I'll put you in the car and drive you back to the house,' Grant told him, as George began, tentatively, to straighten up.

But he could only go so far and, obviously in too much pain to argue, he allowed Grant to lead him to the car and settle him in the front seat.

'Sitting's going to hurt far worse than standing,' the older man said, the words coming out through pain-whitened lips.

'It won't be for long, and it will save Mrs Barrett having to come back and forth to feed you. You need bed rest for a week,' he added, though he knew he might just as well tell the rain to stop. Farmers worked when they had to, whether they were in pain or not.

Though the rain might keep George indoors for longer than he would normally stay.

'I know you won't take any notice of me,' Grant continued, pulling up at the bottom of the steps but not moving. If they waited, the rain might lessen and the drug would have more time to work. 'But try to rest it as long as you can. And no rubbish about lying on the floor because a hard surface is good for backs—that's not right and you'll do more damage getting up and down to go to the toilet than you would lying on the softest of beds. I'll check out your bed, and show you how to lie.'

'You're really Doug's boy? I heard your dad passed away. I'm sorry, he was a good man.'

George was obviously feeling less pain if he'd been able to think of something else. It was as good a time as any to tell him he'd need an X-ray.

'You'll do it or the woman?' George asked, the suspicion in his voice confirming what Katie had said about the older men's reaction to her position as the local GP.

'Actually, whoever is the technician at the hospital will do it, but Dr Fenton and I will read it. After all, she is your doctor. I'm just temporary.'

George muttered something Grant took to be disgust at a world so changed a man had to be treated by a woman doctor, but before Grant could ask for him to repeat it, Mrs Barrett appeared, a large umbrella held above her head.

'I'm already wet so I'll come around and help you out,' he told George. 'Sit tight for a moment.'

He met Mrs Barrett at the car door and opened it, then leaned in to take George's legs.

'I'll swing them out then help you stand,' he told his patient, who was grumbling under his breath, but more, Grant realised, with disgust at himself than with pain.

Together, he and Mrs Barrett got the man onto his bed.

'You can lie on either side with your hips and legs flexed, or on your back but propped up and with pillows under your knees. I'll leave some tablets here to keep you going over the weekend and a script for more, should you need them, for next week.'

Grant turned to Mrs Barrett.

'He'll probably be more comfortable in pyjamas. Do you want some help undressing him?'

She laughed.

'Me need help to undress him? Get away with you, young Grant! I've been undressing the useless hulk for years. Every Friday night it used to be, until drink-driving meant he couldn't drink at the pub till closing time. But I haven't forgotten how,' she added.

'It wasn't that I couldn't do it myself, young fella,' George put in. 'Just she was always desperate to get at my body!'

Grant found himself chuckling at the ribald exchange, though the depth of affection behind it reminded him of his parents' conversations, and the love they'd shared.

And, just as his enforced holiday at Byron Bay had seemed curiously flat once he'd settled in and relaxed, now he wondered if it wasn't perhaps his entire life that was lacking something.

Surely not because he needed someone with whom to share a joke—someone to tease and be teased by?

Though there was no guarantee marriage would provide the answer—he'd already learnt that lesson.

'I want some X-rays to check on what's happening in that lumbar region,' he told Mrs Barrett. 'But wait until he's well enough to travel. In the meantime, if you can keep him in bed, well and good. If you can't then walking—just gentle upright movement—is better than sitting.'

George began growling again, and Mrs Barrett, after telling him to hush, led Grant out of the bedroom.

'Four-hourly for the tablets?' she asked, as Grant dug through the bag again to find some analgesics.

'Yes, but once the effects of the injection wear off, these

mightn't be enough. I'll leave a couple of Valium as well, which will relax the muscles and sedate him slightly. He can take one tonight and another in the morning. If the pain hasn't eased by tomorrow evening, call me again and I'll come out.'

Bursitis was another possibility, he was thinking, as he said goodbye to Mrs Barrett and again ran through the rain. Then, as he settled behind the wheel in the unfamiliar vehicle, he grinned to himself.

It was like riding a bicycle, the way it all came back. Though he wouldn't tell Katie how long it was since he'd done any general medical work. She'd only worry.

Katie!

He drove back thinking about her, replacing the mental picture he'd carried with him for so long—of a skinny, restless teenager—with one of the tall, well-built woman she'd become. Though the wild untamed hair was still the same, and the eyes, if anything, were larger and more luminous, so expressive he'd once believed he could read every thought she ever had. Her skin was pale, but that was understandable, given she was probably exhausted, and everyone was aware these days of the damage sun could do. Though the young Katie had laughed off such warnings and had tanned to a golden glow every summer.

Then he remembered how the baby—Katie's baby—had felt in his hands, and his mood darkened. Had he been foolish to say yes to Aunt Vi's pleas and persuasion?

He was happy to help out—more than happy, given how boring he'd found his 'holiday' and how much he'd wanted to return to Testament, in spite of his teenage vows. He was even happy at the thought of helping Katie, who'd been a close childhood friend, at first thrown at him by his father— 'Be nice to the kid. I'll need all the help I can get from her dad if we're to survive' —but later as a friend in her own right.

More than a friend for a brief few weeks of summer heat and raging teenage testosterone...

His body stirred at the ancient memory and he wondered if he wasn't better thinking of the baby.

As long as he didn't get fond of it...

Though that was unlikely, given Katie's protective attitude and the fact he'd only be here a few weeks, six or seven at the most.

The rain had eased by the time he drove back into the town. He passed the pub and considered stopping for a beer, then remembered he was, more or less, on duty and resisted the impulse. Turned towards the hospital and was surprised to feel a slight anticipatory thrill—actually, more a nudge than a thrill. To do with being back at work, he was sure, not with seeing Katie.

The back door was open, making the dash from garage to house less hazardous, though now the rain had settled into a reasonable kind of splatter, and he was damp, not soaked, when he came through the door.

'Chlorinda's shirt's been more wet than dry this afternoon,' Katie greeted him, and he very nearly blew his neat idea by asking, Who's Chlorinda?

'I'll take it off—have a shower if that's OK with you. I gave George a shot of morphine, got him from the shed to bed, and left Mrs B. ravishing his body.'

Katie's eyebrows rose, but she must have decided not to go there, asking instead, 'Did you leave medication? Ask him to come in for further investigation?' The green eyes darkened with worry. 'I'm not sure about this locum stuff. I mean, do you resent me asking how you've treated someone? Even though the person will still be my patient later, so I'll have to know? In a group practice, notes are written on the patient cards, but it always seemed to me, although they said what the patient had come in for and how the doctor had treated it, a lot of personal but helpful stuff could be missing.'

Grant moved towards her, aware of how attractive she looked, freshly showered, and clad in a long skirt of some clingy, shiny material and a plain green T-shirt hanging out over it. Her hair, which she'd tried to tame by ramming combs into it to hold it somewhere near the top of her head, was escaping in long corkscrew curls.

'You never did have that cup of tea,' he said, 'and though Mrs Barrett offered sustenance, I refused. Let's sit and talk about it, shall we? I can shower later. I certainly don't mind you asking what I did, or how I treated someone—asking anything, in fact. Believe me, I'll be asking heaps of questions myself. It's a long time since I've done a locum, though three years in A and E has prepared me well for the kind of thing you'd get called out for.'

'Prepared you well for anything,' Kate said, concealing a shudder as she remembered some of the bizarre cases she'd experienced in a far shorter stint in Accident and Emergency, as part of her training. 'You sit, I'll make the tea. I've made some scones as well. I'm not good at scones, but if you've reasonable digestion, they're a bit of solid nourishment to carry you through to dinner-time.'

'You made scones?' The words shot across the room, propelled by such incredulity she might have said she'd won the lottery.

'You don't have to sound so surprised!' Kate fired right back at him. 'After all, you don't know me. People do grow up, you know. Now, do you want tea and scones or don't you?'

He nodded and dropped into a chair by the table, in the easy, loose-limbed way she remembered from the past.

Turning resolutely away from loose-limbed movement and memories of the past, she made a pot of tea and plonked it on the table, unhooked two mugs from their wooden holder and put them beside the pot, then lifted the tea-towel off the scones and tried to tell herself she'd meant to make them small.

But when they made clunking noises as she put them on the plate, she sighed.

'You'll need good teeth as well as good digestion,' she admitted, looking into familiar blue eyes that held an even more familiar understanding.

Which prompted her to confess, 'You were right to be surprised—I'm still no cook. You know, Grant, I actually thought skills like making scones might come along with motherhood but, from the look and taste of these, it's another of those myths, like instant bonding.'

A puzzled expression swept away the understanding.

'Instant bonding?'

'With the baby,' she explained, pleased to have someone other than herself with whom to debate this strange occurrence. 'I thought, because I'd given birth to her, I'd have some instant affinity for the wee thing. Go all warm and protective and filled with overwhelming love.'

He still looked puzzled but his easy grin was longing to appear—she could tell by the little twitches at the corner of his mouth.

'Didn't happen, huh?'

Kate shook her head, the movement causing more bits of hair to come floating free, which added frustration with her looks to her gloomy mood.

'She couldn't have been more alien. I mean, I didn't hate her or hold her responsible for anything that's happened, and I still want her and love her to bits, but in the beginning it was like having a stranger come into my life.'

She paused, then added, 'For ever!' in such tragic tones, Grant lost his battle with his amusement and not only grinned but laughed out loud.

'I've often wondered about the bonding thing,' he finally admitted, accepting the mug of tea she pushed in his direction and picking up one of the scones. 'Nature usually gets it right, and maybe it makes human infants so totally dependent to give the parents time to bond. I mean, most newborn animals can almost fend for themselves at birth. Admittedly, mammals need milk but they get up and go find it.'

He cut the scone, with difficulty, and reached for the jam.

'Use plenty. It softens them and masks the taste,' Katie said, and he laughed again, assuring her the scones couldn't be that bad.

'They are,' she told him, and when he took a bite, he had to agree.

'But it doesn't matter,' he told her. 'Setting yourself motherhood goals like instant bonding and scone-making is setting yourself up for failure, Katie. My mother couldn't make scones and she was a country wife of whom it was expected, and a great mother—still is, in fact. And my bond with her, though it may have been dependence-based originally, is now one of loving friendship—of respect, which I hope, from time to time, is mutual.'

'Kate.' She corrected her name, though absent-mindedly, continuing with her main train of thought when she said, 'Your mother's different. She was never a scone sort of mother.'

She looked wistfully at Grant.

'Perhaps I should use her as a role model rather than mine, who sent the scone recipe, along with various others—including of all things, a sponge cake—within a week of my shifting back to Testament.'

Grant grinned at her.

'As if you were expected to start the transformation to Katie—sorry, Kate—the perfect countrywoman, as soon as you started breathing country air.'

His words prompted another thought—why wasn't her mother here, supporting her at this time? But she was looking less distressed and he didn't want to chase that mood away just yet.

He bit into the jam-loaded scone and chewed carefully.

'You know, the Americans call scones biscuits, and if

you call it a biscuit, it's perfect, just the right amount of chew and hardness.'

That won a smile, of sorts, but he could see the sadness lurking in her eyes and wondered what had happened to his brave, confident, daring, laughing Katie to turn her into this uncertain woman.

Not wanting to ask, he told her about his visit to the Barretts'—what he'd done, prescribed and suggested.

'If we have time each day to talk over the patients, we shouldn't have any trouble keeping track of what's going on.'

She nodded. 'That's one of the reasons I wanted the locum to live in.'

The doubt in her voice told him she no longer considered it quite as good an idea.

'Very sensible arrangement all round,' he said, hoping a firm confirmation might banish some of her doubts. 'And though I'm not a woman, I'm quite capable of watching over a small baby when you're working or want to go out.'

That drew a smile.

'Out on the town, you mean?' Katie—Kate—teased. 'Hitting the high spots of Testament?'

He answered with his own smile, then added, 'You still need time for yourself. Even perfect mothers need that.'

She nodded as if she knew it was true, but her eyes told him she didn't—well, not entirely—believe it.

'I think perfect is way beyond my reach,' she admitted. 'Right now, I'd settle for adequate.'

She leaned back in her chair, put her hands behind her head and stretched, then sighed.

'Almost adequate?'

Unable to believe she could have had so much stuffing knocked out of her—it had to be the man, the father, who'd so undermined her confidence—Grant was about to go into confidence-building speak when a faint cry alerted both of them to the fact the baby was once again awake.

'I'll get her, you stay there and rest,' Grant said, leaping to his feet so quickly he knocked over the chair.

But Katie was up just as quickly, taking advantage of him having to right the chair, so she beat him to the door, where she turned to say, 'Nonsense! Even almost adequate mothers can do the changing-feeding thing. There's no reason why you should be chasing after her.'

He followed anyway, and saw colour return to the pale cheeks as Katie leaned over the crib, murmuring quietly as she lifted the wrapped bundle out and snuggled her momentarily against her shoulder.

Fascinated by this maternal and obviously baby-doting Katie—he'd be damned if he'd call her Kate—he settled on the far side of the big queen-sized bed and watched as she lowered the baby onto the bed, then turned to sort through the paraphernalia he'd investigated earlier.

'We haven't been properly introduced, your daughter and I,' he said, making conversation while he watched her hands fumble through the still unfamiliar task of removing the wet nappy. He leaned forward and inserted his forefinger into one tiny hand, knowing the little fingers would grip his larger one. Wanting to feel that grip again. 'I'm Grant Bell,' he said formally. 'And you're...'

He glanced up at Katie, expecting an answer, and found her frowning ferociously at him.

'Don't ask!' she warned.

'You haven't named her?' he guessed, then wished he'd managed to sound a little less disbelieving.

Kate pushed her fingers through her now riotous hair and knew she'd have to at least try to explain.

'It was like the bonding thing—you know, instant motherhood? I thought when she was born I'd take one look and say, Hello Annabel, or Rachel, or Sophie or whatever it was she looked like. Or he'd look like if she'd been a he. I thought I'd *know*!'

'But you had nine months to think about names. Didn't

you have a few you rather fancied all ready for hers and his? Don't most people make a list?'

'Don't talk to me about lists!' she said, injecting the words with enough venom to stop even someone as insensitive as Grant Bell had apparently become. 'If one more person suggests lists, makes a list or sends me a list, I won't be answerable for the consequences.'

Then, aware she'd raised her voice, causing what looked like wariness in her daughter's large blue eyes, she completed the nappy change, lifted the infant and said, more quietly, 'I'm going to feed her now.'

Grant made no attempt to leave the room. In fact, if anything, he looked as if he was settling himself more comfortably on the bed.

Her bed.

'In here,' she added, because it seemed kind of prissy to be asking him outright to leave the room.

'That's OK,' he told her in a genial voice she recognised from their schooldays. It meant he understood but didn't necessarily agree.

This reading of his vocal nuances was confirmed when he added, 'I love watching babies nurse. There's something so wholeheartedly selfish about it. They tug and pummel away at their poor mothers' breasts, with no thought for anything but the acute physical satisfaction of being replete.'

'Well, this poor mother would prefer to have her breast tugged and pummelled in private,' Kate told him.

'You mean you haven't fed her in front of anyone yet? What about in hospital? Or at work? Vi said you were planning on taking her to the surgery and whoever was there would mind her between feeds. Hasn't that happened yet? Or do you let them do the dirty work of changing nappies and burping but don't let them have the satisfaction of watching her feed?'

'You make it sound like a rare treat for all concerned,'

Kate said crossly. 'I'll have you know a lot of people are still offended by seeing women breastfeed in public, and though I'd defend to my dying breath their right to do it, it isn't my thing. Not yet, anyway.'

She gave him a glare that should put him back in his place—though she wasn't entirely certain where that was—and added, in case he hadn't got the message, 'So go! Unpack. Check out the surgery. Do something, anything, just not here.'

CHAPTER THREE

GRANT walked back to the kitchen, and wondered what to do next. A shower was the obvious answer, but Katie's behaviour—the vulnerability he sensed beneath her usual confident manner, made him wonder about the baby's father—and about how much she might be hurting inside.

Vi might know something, but asking Vi seemed like a betrayal—as if he'd be going behind his old friend's back. He put off the shower, mooching through the house instead, not exactly searching but seeking some hint as to the identity of this man.

Not that it was any of his business, he told himself, when the only photos sitting on her study desk proved to be of her parents.

Which made him wonder again where they were and why her mother wasn't helping out with the new baby.

His heart clenched with concern for his old friend and, realising that wasn't a good way to be feeling, given that his stay in Testament was definitely short term, he sought about for a diversion. Maybe he should have that shower!

Though it was still raining outside, so perhaps he should check out the surgery first. Providing he could find the keys…

They were in the kitchen, labelled, should anyone break in looking for them, SURGERY. The set-up was as he remembered—a consulting room and opposite it a small treatment room were set behind the main reception and waiting areas. A small locked room must hold medical supplies while the other store cupboards held such an accumulation of junk that he wondered if any of the doctors who'd served the town had ever thrown anything out. Sorting through it was a bit like going to a medical museum, and he was so caught up in the treasures it wasn't until it became too dark to see that he realised how long he'd been there. He packed everything back in, but not before promising himself he'd sort it out properly one day.

One day? You're only temporary, he reminded himself, so it's none of your business.

By the time Grant returned to the house, the storm had passed, and a glance at his watch told him it was after six, while his stomach reminded him it was a long time since he'd eaten, if you didn't count a biscuity scone. Presumably the woman locum would have shared responsibility for meal preparation. Well, that was OK. He could rustle up a meal for the two of them.

He opened the refrigerator and peered inside.

There wasn't a lot to see. The remains of a dubious-looking casserole someone must have left for Katie, cosied up to two wrinkled apples and a loaf of bread. She did, however, have four litres of milk and a couple of small feeding bottles of what he assumed was expressed breast milk.

He tried the freezer next and winced at the neat stack of frozen meals. Pushed them aside, and continued searching. There had to be real food here somewhere.

There wasn't.

Forgetting his decision to present a professional demeanour, he stalked back to the bedroom where, noticing the baby had dropped off to sleep in her arms, he delivered his tirade in a loud whisper.

Kate heard the words—nothing to eat, bad nutrition, looking after herself, thinking about the baby—and the kindly thoughts she'd been thinking about Grant Bell dried up.

'It wasn't my fault the baby came early,' she told him, standing up so she could fight him toe to toe. 'She was supposed to come in a fortnight, on the Friday, last Friday, and I'd intended shopping before that. Then I'd have had the weekend in hospital to rest, and with the locum here, she could have started on the Monday, tomorrow, and I could have worked part time during the week. But the baby was early and the locum wasn't here, and the shopping wasn't done...'

She stopped, aware she was repeating herself and, even worse, sounding self-pitying. Better to attack.

'And for your information, those frozen meals are very well balanced, nutritionally.'

'Ho!' Grant scoffed. 'Don't tell me you believe what's written on the packet.'

She was about to tell him about labelling laws when she realised they'd got way off the subject. And though she hated to admit it, the meals left her feeling unsatisfied, so they'd never do for Grant for his dinner.

Checking the time on the bedside clock, she realised the store would be closed and she had no time to retrieve the situation.

'We can have Chinese take-aways tonight, and I'll shop tomorrow,' she suggested, settling the baby in the crib and leading the way out of the bedroom so if, or when, they argued again, they wouldn't wake the little one. 'Though I don't know what good that will do,' she added honestly. 'I'm not much better at meal-cooking than I am at scones. I can grill chops or steak or sausages, steam vegetables and mash potatoes, but nothing fancy.'

Grant smiled.

'I can do the fancy stuff,' he told her. 'We'll take turns, shall we? And we'll both shop tomorrow. That way we can get what we need and the baby can have an outing.'

'Both shop? Together?'

Kate knew it made sense, but the idea bothered her.

'Worried what people might think?' Grant asked.

'No,' she said, too quickly. If she'd thought about it, a

yes would have been better, then he wouldn't persist, as he surely would.

'Why, then?'

He came in right on cue, but she could only shrug as if her worries were inexplicable. Which, to some extent, they were. She could hardly tell him that it seemed too like a family for the three of them to be shopping together. If she came out with something so fatuous within hours of their unexpected reunion, he'd realise just how many brain cells she'd lost.

He didn't ask again, merely picking up the restaurant menu she had stuck on the fridge door and studying the offerings.

'Do you have any particular fancy? Any favourites? I should probably let you choose as you'd know what's good.'

Kate found herself smiling.

'You're asking me? I think frozen meals are good,' she reminded him. 'But I do like the crispy duck. It's loaded with cholesterol-raising fat, but it's so-o-o delicious. I usually have a vegetable dish as well. As a nod to dietary propriety. And lots of rice—that's carbohydrate so, all in all, it's a balanced meal.'

He crossed to the phone and, watching him dial, hearing his deep masculine voice as he ordered, Kate felt a sense of loneliness, as if having Grant here—perhaps anyone here—brought home to her just how alone she'd been these past six months.

'That's set. Now I really will have that shower I've been talking about since I arrived. Then we'll sit down and relax with a long cool drink and tell each other lies about how successful we've become.' He flashed a smile that made her heart falter for a moment. 'Isn't that what medicos usually do when they see each other?'

Kate returned his smile, though she knew hers was more restrained. The faltering-heart thing had shocked her with its intensity. And she wasn't going anywhere near that final question, although it was exactly how Mark had always behaved when he'd met up with fellow doctors.

However, they would have to talk about a lot of other things—work hours, payment, shared expenses for food. She was searching through the bottom of her handbag in the hope of finding enough spare change to pay for the meal when this thought struck her. Generally locums took over while the doctor was away, so the question of expenses didn't arise. Why were there no rules for the little things in life?

So many little things—like bathroom etiquette in a shared house.

'I've been thinking about names,' Grant announced, reappearing far too quickly for her peace of mind and looking, in another flower-festooned shirt and red board shorts this time, incredibly laidback and devastatingly handsome. 'We could think of a few—a few isn't a list—then try them out on her. Use one one week and another the next to see which fits best.'

She ignored her physical reactions to the devastatingly handsome bit, and should have told him the baby's name was none of his business, but the idea of changing names on a weekly basis was so far out, she went for that instead.

'Couldn't it do her irreparable harm, to call her Sophie one week then Louise the next? And I can't have Louise, which I quite like, because I've decided to use "Jeez Louise" as an expletive so she doesn't say "Damn" as her first utterance.'

Grant seemed to understand this reasoning, which, when she actually said it, sounded weird to Kate, but when he spoke she realised he'd probably ignored most of what she'd said.

'You mentioned Sophie before—do you like it? Is she starting to look like a Sophie?'

Kate sighed.

'That's just the problem,' she said. 'I can see a grown-up Sophie—even a teenage Sophie—but as a name for a little tiny baby? It sounds too mature somehow.'

She spoke so earnestly Grant knew he had to hide the smile that was his reaction to her statement.

'I can see your point. Like Jack—one of my nephews. I always thought it a great name for a grown man, but a little harsh for a newborn.' He looked across the table to where Katie, for all her dislike of lists, appeared to be making one. 'But you do get used to it. It's my experience that babies grow into their names.'

Kate glanced up at him, the green eyes sweeping across his face as if trying to read messages on it.

'Are you humouring me?'

He shook his head.

'Now, why would I do that?'

'Because I'm disorganised and possibly neurotic and haven't any food in the house?' she suggested. 'I also haven't any cash to pay for the meal, and I have no idea how to organise your pay or our shared expenses or who uses the bathroom first, so you could add disorganised to my failings.'

She gave a huge sigh, blinked back all but one escaping tear, swiped at it, then sniffed.

'You know, Grant, people talk about the baby blues. I've even said to weepy post-partum mothers, "Don't worry, dear, it happens to most new mums." But I never for a minute thought I'd go to pieces like this.'

He walked around the table and pulled a chair close so he could put his arm around her shoulder.

'From what I've seen and heard, you have every right to go to pieces. Sophie arrived before you were ready for her, you've had to manage the whole pregnancy on your own and juggle work commitments at the same time. And being Katie Fenton, I bet if anyone offered help, you refused it.'

She gave him a watery smile.

'Vi brought a casserole. I accepted that,' she said.

She hesitated, then added, 'Actually, a lot of people have been very nice to me. But they don't run any antenatal classes here because most of the women go to Craigtown for their babies. Paul Newberry—he was the hospital doctor when I arrived—preferred not to deliver babies, claiming it was too risky without a specialist in town, and while he didn't actually refuse to do obstetrics work, his attitude was enough to put most women off.'

'You mentioned his name earlier—I gather he's now the ex-hospital doctor.'

'He left six weeks ago. His wife left first—not long after I arrived. Apparently she couldn't stand the country. Then he suddenly disappeared without a word to the board, or me, or anyone, as far as I know.'

'So who did you see for your pregnancy check-ups?'

'Paul!' A defiant glint in her eyes suggested it hadn't been easy to get him to agree to this arrangement, but before Grant could comment she added, 'And, no, I don't think the imminent arrival of my baby was what forced him out of town, although to hear some of the nursing staff talk, you'd wonder. Anyway, although he wasn't happy doing the checks, he did them until he left, though he never talked about what to expect—the tiredness all the time, this weepy business. To be fair to him, I guess he thought I knew it all.'

'And being an independent spirit, you did nothing to disabuse him of this notion,' Grant muttered as the true extent of Katie's isolation struck home.

She sighed, then shook her head.

'You know, I came back here because I remembered being so happy and secure here. When things changed and I needed somewhere to establish myself and the baby—somewhere I could make a safe, stable, happy life for the two of us and at the same time give something back to the community—by chance the practice was for sale. Serendipity,

I thought. But breaking back into a country town isn't easy.'

'Give the locals time,' Grant said, withdrawing his arm because holding her was making him think things he shouldn't think—suggesting perhaps he could kiss away her despair. 'Country folk take a while to make up their minds, but once they accept you, you've friends for life. And you have to remember your position sets you a little apart. Most people feel doctors are entitled to respect.'

'Respect? When the entire town remembers me as the girl who danced naked on top of the water tower? I'd actually forgotten that until I came back and the first patient I saw mentioned it.'

She shifted back in her chair, the better to glare at him.

'And no one seems to remember it was your fault, anyway. You dared me to do it—well, maybe not to dance, but to climb up to the top and take my clothes off.'

'I didn't think you'd do it,' Grant protested, remembering the skinny eleven-year-old who'd not only taken the dare but had capered naked about the top of the tower until her father had appeared on the street below and ordered her down.

'How is your father, by the way? And your mother? Both parents well?' he asked, as thinking of her parents reminded him of the lack of support for Katie. Illness might have prevented them coming out to be with her at this time.

'Conversational switch, but I can see why you thought of my father,' she acknowledged. 'They're both well. Though, with my usual lack of judgement, I managed to have a baby right in the middle of my father's long-service leave. They'd planned a trip around the world—talked about it for years—and finally had it all booked and paid for when I discovered I was pregnant. They wanted to cancel it, but I couldn't let them do that.'

The words were clipped, and suggested something else was bothering her as far as her parents were concerned.

He raised his eyebrows, and waited.

'Mum wanted me to have an abortion and couldn't understand why not, especially as Mark wanted to marry me.'

Mark? She'd been involved with someone called Mark? Terrible name.

Then Grant put aside his strange reaction to hearing Sophie's father's name and followed another puzzle.

'Why did she want you to have an abortion if Mark wanted to marry you?'

Katie's green eyes met his and a flicker of what must have been remembered temper flared briefly.

'Mark wanted it, too. He had a list,' she said flatly, as if she'd ironed all the emotion out of the subject long ago. 'First abortion, second engagement, third decide what specialty I should pursue, and finally, if I behaved myself and toed the line—or should that be followed the instructions—we'd get married.'

Grant frowned and shook his head.

'I must have missed something. He wanted you to have an abortion when you were getting married anyway?'

'So it didn't look as if we'd had to get married. In fact, on the list, babies came way down—ninth or tenth if I remember rightly.'

Her voice was so husky he suspected not quite all the emotion had been ironed out, particularly where babies were concerned. But another item on the list puzzled him as well.

'And what about number three? Choose your specialty? Did you want to specialise? And was it any of his business, even if you did get married, what you chose?'

The eyes flashed sparks again.

'Exactly!' Katie said, straightening in her chair and looking more like the fighter he'd known in the past. Then she chuckled. 'Actually, I can see his side of things. I must have driven him nuts, doing dribs of this and drabs of that. When I actually sat down and thought about it, although

I'd always said I was doing the short courses—you know, the ones in Obs and Gyn, anaesthesia, surgery—to try them out before specialising, I realised I was preparing myself for something entirely different—for general practice and country general practice at that.'

She looked across at Grant and smiled so warmly he felt a jolt like an electrical current run through his body, causing a muscle spasm in his heart.

'Remember Dr Darling? When we lived in Testament, even though there was always a hospital doctor, Dr Darling did everything for his patients—delivered the babies, diagnosed problems, whipped out the odd appendix, the lot. I realised that's what I wanted to be, not just a token doctor but someone people could rely on—an old-fashioned kind of doctor with the welfare of the community and each individual at heart.'

He heard the commitment in her voice, and saw it shining in her eyes, and for a moment envied the passion she had for this dream she was pursuing. And though he had commitment by the bucketload, he hadn't felt the fire of passion since he'd given up his dream of buying back the farm.

'So you saw yourself as another Dr Darling?' he teased, when he realised it was his turn in the conversation. But as he said the words, warning bells clanged furiously in his head.

Watch yourself, linking words like that, his common sense warned.

'Was that Sophie?' he asked, because Katie was looking at him as if the words had startled her as well and he wanted to divert her attention. 'I thought I heard a cry.'

'Her name's not Sophie, you know,' she said—showing the diversion had worked. 'You can't just walk in here, pull a name out of a hat and give it to my baby.'

'I didn't pull it out of a hat,' Grant protested. 'You mentioned it twice yourself. I'm happy for you to choose something else, even on a temporary basis, but we can't keep calling her "hey, you" or "the baby".'

A mulish expression, familiar from their shared youth, settled on Katie's features.

'I don't see why not!' Kate said crisply, determined to put Grant Bell in his place, then a knock on the front door put paid to this plan. She'd have to borrow money to pay for the meal, which was a little awkward if one had just been rude to the only available funding source.

'I'll get it. We'll work out the financial ramifications later,' Grant said, and walked away before she could object. Then the phone rang.

'Single vehicle accident out on the highway,' Narelle Speares, the nurse covering A and E at the hospital, said. 'One person, the driver, in the vehicle. The ambulance is on the way out, with an ETA back at the hospital of an hour. I'll give you a call when I get a definite time, but I thought you might like the extra warning to organise the baby.'

'Thanks, Narelle. I appreciate that. I'll call Tara now.'

She was still standing by the phone, uncertainty nibbling at her confidence, when Grant returned with a plastic bag trailing the tantalising whiff of delicious food.

'Called out just as dinner hits the table?' he asked, and she realised he'd have heard the phone.

'No, I've time for dinner.' She explained briefly but still hovered by the phone.

'I'll take the accident case when it comes in,' Grant said. 'After all, it's right up my alley. Three years in A and E, remember.'

He'd found plates and set them on the table and was now opening the plastic containers, releasing more saliva-producing aromas, but Kate still hesitated.

'Come and eat,' Grant urged. 'I'm starving and I can't start without you.'

'I'm coming,' Kate assured him, then she lifted the receiver and dialled Tara's number.

'Hi, Tara, it's Kate. Dr Fenton. Could you pop over in an hour and watch the baby for me?'

She accepted Tara's assurances she'd be there, if not with relief then with less concern than usual, and sat down opposite Grant.

'And Tara is?' he asked.

'A year-twelve student who babysits. She's very obliging, comes in at night or weekends, stays over if she needs to and doesn't charge the earth.'

'And why are you so uncertain about this paragon?'

'I am not!' Kate retorted, but knew from his snort of disbelief she hadn't said it firmly enough. 'She's easily distracted,' she admitted. 'Wants to study medicine, and will start a science degree as a preliminary next year. She loves to read and the problem is, once she's stuck into a book—even something as boring as *Principles of Medicine*—she loses track of time and place.'

'So you sometimes wonder if she loses track of a baby crying as well?'

Kate nodded.

'Though she's very good with the baby. She calls her "little scrap". I really should do something about a name, or the poor thing *will* get confused.'

Grant saw Katie's forehead furrow with worry and wanted to reach out to smooth the pale skin, then he remembered why he was here, ate some more food and asked the question he should have asked before getting sidetracked onto Tara.

'If I'm going over to meet the ambulance, why are you organising a sitter for Sophie?'

He knew by the swift frown that Katie was about to argue the 'Sophie' thing, but then a more important matter apparently took over and she smiled.

'I thought we could both go. Or that I'd make arrangements so we'd both be available if needed. It's such a great opportunity, Grant, to prove that country hospitals can do far more than stabilising patients and sending them on to a regional centre, which is all Paul Newberry ever felt obliged to do. I honestly believe that's happening too much and it's detrimental to patient welfare, as well as being inconvenient and often downright disruptive to the family. With you here, if the patient has injuries a simple operation can fix, we can do it, with one of us acting as anaesthetist and the other as surgeon.'

'We're not talking major stuff here, are we?' Grant asked, pleased to see Katie so enthusiastic but dubious about tackling too big a job with the limited facilities of a small country hospital at their disposal.

'No!' she snapped, so crossly he guessed she'd argued this before. 'I'm talking about suturing or setting simple fractures, things a small hospital should be able to manage. I read back through old hospital files when I first came here, and a young man, injured in a fall from a horse on a Picnic Race day, died on the way to hospital, when a burr hole might have saved him.'

'Burr holes I can do,' Grant assured her, 'though let's hope this patient doesn't need one. Eat up. I see your point. We're getting back to Dr Darling, aren't we? To doctors in those days doing far more varied work within their practice and the hospital.'

Kate forked up some food, savoured the taste for a moment, then leapt back into the conversation.

'Exactly! Even in Dr Darling's time, Testament used to have a series of young doctors at the hospital for a year, or in some cases less than that, so people relied on him far more than they would otherwise. Then, when Dr Darling retired, and the practice became vacant, I suppose the hospital doctor became too busy to do much more than stabilise people and send them on. I guess it was inevitable the hospital became a kind of rehab centre for patients after they'd been treated elsewhere.'

'So how does all this affect your grand plan?' he asked, amused by the enthusiasm lighting her eyes and deepening her voice.

'To be the world's best single mother and country doctor?' She grinned at him. 'Disastrously, that's how. At the moment, the first ambition seems like an impossible dream—even adequate's a battle—and as for doctoring... Once Paul left, and even before the baby arrived, I was flat out keeping up with the extra responsibilities at the hospital on top of my own work, so I haven't had a moment to think about, let alone organise, things like well-patient clinics and all the other ancillary things I think a country GP could do.'

Kate paused, savouring the taste of the food, while her mind whirled with the ideas she'd been unable to share.

Until now.

'If we can get some stability into the hospital position, then I know I can convince the board and nursing staff it's worthwhile to do more here. Obstetrics would be a start. And most of the nurses would be happy to have more challenging work than they're currently doing. Several have expressed interest in doing further training, especially in anaesthesia.'

'Most of the nurses?' Grant echoed, and watched her wide, full lips twist into a grimace.

'Remember Sister Clarke who did the sex-education lectures when we were at school? The ones that made me even more confused than your lecture on how cattle did it?'

Grant chuckled, but felt his body respond to the question, remembering more the demonstration than the lecture.

'Well, she's still here and more than happy with the status quo. She's one year off retirement and doesn't want any hassles. In fact, the fewer really sick people she has in the hospital, the happier she is. A couple of weeks ago she wanted to send old Ma Chisholm to Craigtown because of a simple case of pneumonia, which cleared up in a few days when treated with IV antibiotics. Poor old Ma cried when Sister Clarke suggested it, and I had a no doubt much-talked-about argument with Sister before insisting Ma stay.'

'Did you yell?' Grant asked, remembering how Kate's voice had always got louder and louder as she'd argued.

'Just a bit!' she admitted, smiling at him across the table. 'I was having labour pains at the time, so I wasn't at my most conciliatory. Though I did try being nice to start off with.'

'I can imagine,' Grant said, smiling as he pictured the confrontation between the pregnant woman and the formidable old nursing sister. 'But I can understand what you're saying. It's better, especially for the sake of the patient's family, for people to be treated close to home, though the clustering of specialist services in larger hospitals has reduced the opportunity for that to happen.'

'I think we're getting over-specialised,' Katie said, her ready enthusiasm firing colour into her cheeks. 'Look at orthopaedics, where you have knee, hip, hand and probably even finger sub-specialties. And are patients getting better service? I don't think so.'

Grant, determinedly ignoring the attractiveness of pink cheeks, was about to point out that in some cases they probably were, but the phone rang and someone tapped on the front door, then footsteps in the hall suggested Tara felt enough at home to come straight in.

'The ambulance should be there in ten minutes.' Katie put down the receiver and turned to welcome Tara with a smile and a hug.

'This is Grant Bell—your parents would remember his family. He's gone from being the town bad boy to a respectable doctor, or so he tells me, and he'll be taking most of my calls.'

'So you won't need me to mind the little scrap as often?' Tara said, in such tragic tones that Katie laughed.

'You can come and read my books any time,' she offered, and Grant saw the affection in her eyes as she looked at the young student. 'Admit it—they're the attraction, not a boring baby. Speaking of which, there's milk for her in the refrigerator, and we'll just be at the hospital. We mightn't be long, depending on what we find.'

'Katie mightn't be long—I'm supposed to be the one on call,' Grant added, but Tara was already moving off towards the study.

'She seems keen,' he said, as Katie led the way out the back door where a concrete path crossed to the back of the hospital.

'And starved for reading material,' Kate told him. 'As soon as she heard I was pregnant she offered her services, free, as a babysitter, which was comforting as I'd been trying, without much success, to find someone who'd be willing to come in on a daily basis once the baby arrived.'

'But if she's at school, she can't do that,' Grant said, trying to make sense of the arrangement.

'I *know* that!' Katie told him, coming to a halt at the back of the hospital. 'I had this weird idea that finding someone to look after a small baby would be easy.' She grinned at him. 'Easy-peasy, in fact,' she said, using the phrase she'd always used in her childhood. 'But, boy, was I wrong. I'm quite convinced that some people, if they can't be brain surgeons or super IT company bosses, don't want to work at all. So, at the moment, the baby comes to the surgery with me during the day. Vi and Sally, the clerk, mind her there while I'm working, then evenings and weekends I've got Tara.'

'Who might or might not hear the baby cry, depending on how engrossed she is in the alimentary system or whatever else she's reading up on.'

'Exactly,' Katie said, then, as the approaching siren grew

louder, she walked up the ramp and in through the rear entrance of the hospital.

'It smells the same as it did when I broke my leg when I was twelve, and was in traction for four weeks of the summer holidays.'

Katie nodded.

'I thought the same the minute I walked into the place, and at first assumed it was just a hospital smell, but then I realised it's hospital mixed with oleanders—the line of shrubs on the other boundary. Though why anyone would plant something as potentially deadly as oleanders in hospital grounds is a mystery to me.'

Grant sniffed again, not able to distinguish anything except familiarity.

Kate looked at him, standing there in the brightly lit doorway, sniffing the air with the same intensity he'd always done most things.

Familiarity! That's all that's unsettling you, she told herself, though other bits of her knew it was more to do with the way his body had matured, and the twinkle in his blue eyes when he smiled at her, as if she was somehow special.

But they'd twinkled the same way at Tara, and without much effort she could recall the name of several high school girls who'd thought that twinkle had been just for them.

'Come and meet people,' she said, aware the sirens had stopped and their patient had arrived. Then she remembered it had been Narelle who'd phoned.

Boy, were Grant's eyes about to twinkle when he saw the tall brunette.

For a moment, Kate regretted bringing him across, though that was stupid. If two doctors could offer better service to the patient, then why not use both of them?

CHAPTER FOUR

KATE watched closely, but though Narelle had the expected effect on Grant, who twinkled away at her, it was Narelle who overdid things, positively gushing with delight to meet the new man in town, though rumour had it she was all but engaged to the recently arrived area agricultural advisor.

And given that Grant was also engaged, shouldn't he be twinkling less?

'Actually, I might have got you here under false pretences,' Narelle said, speaking to Kate but smiling at Grant. 'The lad's car was a write-off but he wasn't badly injured. Concussion and a watching brief, I'd say. Dr Bell could see to him while you go back to the baby.'

It was a blatant dismissal and Kate hesitated, uncertain how to handle it, but when Grant said, 'Don't you trust me, Katie?' she knew she had to go. She could hardly stay and appear to be overseeing his examination of the patient.

Though until a new doctor was appointed, the patients in the hospital were her responsibility, so whether or not Grant—or Narelle—liked it, she would stay.

'As Tara's already minding the baby, I'll just check the patient with you then go through to the office. Catch up on a bit of paperwork,' she said, and led the two of them towards the admitting area.

The patient was, as Narelle had said, not much the worse for wear. Contusions on his face and one arm, and bruises coming out on his skin, but sitting up on the gurney and chatting to the ambulance bearers.

'Gareth Crowe! I might have known!' Kate said as soon as she saw him. 'Well, maybe this is good luck. You can meet the man people are always talking about and comparing you to. Gareth, this is Grant Bell.'

'You're *that* Grant Bell?' Narelle said, eyeing Grant even more lasciviously.

'Hey, are you really?' Gareth asked, putting out his hand then wincing as pain caught him with it half-extended. 'I thought you might have been made up—you know, like the bogeyman. People have been saying "You're just another Grant Bell" to me for so long, I'd started to think you were one of those things they have in books—a myth.'

He studied Grant, taking in the flowered shirt and board shorts, long bare legs and sneakers without socks.

'Did you turn out as bad as people predicted? Are you a beach bum? Did Dr Fenton bring you in to show me how I might end up?'

He grinned at Grant.

'I'm actually a doctor,' Grant told him, and Kate guessed he'd been taken aback by Gareth's questions. 'I was holidaying at Byron Bay when I heard Katie—Dr Fenton—needed a locum, so all I had with me were beach clothes.'

'You're a d-doctor?' Gareth stuttered. 'Like Dr Fenton? Like Tara wants to be?'

Kate chuckled at his astonishment.

'Ordinary people, like Grant and me and Tara—though she's far brighter than Grant and I were at school, so not so ordinary—and even you, do become doctors, you know. It takes a bit of work and study, but most people can make it if they decide it's what they really want to do.'

'Which is a better reason for going into something like medicine than for the money you can make.'

Grant's statement was so un-Grant-like that Kate was temporarily shocked, then she remembered it had been many years since she'd seen him and, however much they might have seemed familiar to each other, she had no idea what kind of man the teenage Grant had grown into.

Neither had she checked he really was a doctor, but as

Vi had brought him back to Testament, and she trusted Vi, who'd run the doctor's surgery since Dr Darling's days, Kate had to assume it was OK.

'I'll leave you to judge what kind of doctor he became,' she said to Gareth, then, determined not to make a fool of herself by hanging around, she walked through to the office where there was a genuine pile of paperwork awaiting her attention.

She had just settled behind her desk and was considering where to start when Narelle appeared.

'Grant says can you come,' she said, and Kate knew from her voice something had gone very wrong.

'Maybe you should have crossed your fingers when you mentioned burr holes,' Grant said, as he helped a wardsman wheel the gurney towards the theatre. They weren't running, or in any other way indicating panic, but they moved with swift purpose. 'Gareth complained briefly of a bad headache then lapsed into unconsciousness again, his systolic pressure's shot up and heartbeat's slowed.'

'Dilated pupil?' Kate asked, knowing a period of unconsciousness followed by a lucid period then a lapse back into coma was usually a sign of an acute epidural haemorrhage.

'Right side. We were about to X-ray his skull for fractures when he deteriorated.'

Grant kept speaking as they moved, and Kate took in what had already been given to the young man. Her mind raced ahead, working out drugs and dosages—always dicey in the case of brain-injured patients.

Though once they'd drilled a hole and released the leaking blood which was causing pressure on Gareth's brain, he should make a full recovery.

If they were quick enough...

'You've done it before?' she asked Grant, and saw his quick nod.

'Then I'll do the anaesthetic and Narelle can assist you.'

She went ahead, entering Theatre through the dressing rooms and hurriedly donning theatre pyjamas over her clothes, exchanging her own sandals for the floppy paper slippers, pulling a cap over her unruly hair and grabbing a mask.

In the theatre itself, she set up the monitor and found the drugs, catheters and tubing she'd need. Narelle came in with a sealed bundle.

'I've seen this burr-hole bundle,' she said as she unwrapped it to expose the instruments and swabs Grant would need, 'but never thought I'd see it used here.'

'Did you check the date on it?' Kate asked, knowing the paper wrappings on the sterile bundle of instruments and swabs could deteriorate, allowing contamination into the bundle.

'It's current,' Narelle assured her. 'All the bundles were changed when Paul arrived—it was one thing he did do.'

Kate wasn't surprised by the remark, as she had yet to hear many positive comments about Paul Newberry. Though, now she considered the urgency, the use-by date on the bundle was irrelevant.

The patient was lifted onto the operating table, and while Narelle and Grant scrubbed Kate readied him for the operation, positioning him on the table with the injured side uppermost, propping his right shoulder on a towel so his head was rotated with the dilated pupil uppermost, draping his body with sterile sheeting and covering all but a small portion of his skull with the green, papery material. She checked the airway Grant must have inserted and made sure its connection to the oxygen supply was clear but out of the way, and that the leads to the monitor were also connected but not about to impair access to the site of the operation.

Working with deft fingers, she inserted a catheter and taped it to the back of Gareth's left hand, then glanced at her watch. It had seemed like ages, but only five minutes earlier he had been talking to them.

She chose an anaesthetising agent which could be easily reversed. Though Gareth was unconscious now, it wouldn't do to have him coming to as the pressure was released during the operation.

Grant and Narelle came in, Narelle taking up her position beside the trolley where the instruments were displayed.

'At least we don't have to shave his head,' Grant remarked. 'No way would we have been allowed at school with shaven heads.'

He was talking as he measured and marked the place where he'd cut, his fingers moving swiftly into position above the lad's temporal area, above the zygomatic arch and behind the ear. With skilful movements for a man not used to surgery, he sliced through the skin, separated the muscle away from the bone, drilled through the skull to the inner surface and changed the drill for a softer burr.

There was no chit-chat, no jokes, all of them aware, without the need for words, that Gareth lived or died depending on the speed and success of what they were doing.

'I'll scoop out a little more soft material then syringe out the blood,' Grant said, and Kate found herself admiring Narelle's efficiency and the smooth way she and Grant worked together.

And wondering why the observation made her feel more grouchy than pleased.

'Suction?'

Kate watched and waited, and even through the loose-fitting theatre garb saw Grant's shoulders relax.

'It's thick, coagulating, nothing fresh and red, so hopefully the little bleeder's shut itself off and we don't have to look any further.'

Kate felt her relief like a physical lightening of weight, though she knew this end stage of the operation was up to her. While Grant patched and stitched the hole he'd made, she had to bring Gareth slowly back to a level just below consciousness, then find a satisfactory means of keeping him sedated enough to make the journey to Craigtown comfortably and with a minimum of distress. Once there, the decision would be made as to whether to keep him in an induced coma for a few days while any swelling in his brain subsided.

'I'll take it from here,' she told Grant. 'He'll have to go to Craigtown for scans and observation so I'll get him ready to transport. His parents are probably here by now, so maybe if you could talk to them? Explain…?'

He'd pulled off his mask as he walked away from the operating table and he turned to smile at Kate.

'You want me to do the dirty work?'

'I do not!' she said indignantly, though the smile had sent a quiver across her skin. 'Anyway, I'd have thought you'd be pleased to see Helen Crowe.' She paused for a beat then, straight-faced, added, 'She was Helen Jones—Miss Jones to you and all the rest of the senior maths class.'

'Our Miss J-Jones?' Grant stuttered, moving his hands in the air to indicate an exaggeratedly hourglass figure.

'The very same,' Kate assured him, smiling at the expression of horror on his face. 'She's Gareth's stepmother.'

'I'll do the reversal,' he offered. 'Take over from you. After all, you're the local doctor, you should talk to them.'

Kate chuckled.

'You're what, nearly thirty-one, and still afraid of your old maths teacher?'

'You may laugh,' Grant said grimly. 'But there wasn't a boy in high school who didn't lust after that woman, but she could cut off your legs and shrivel your—well, you know what she could shrivel, with one glance. Then she'd complete the annihilation by doubling the maths homework.'

He paused then added, 'Actually, it's a wonder we didn't all end up sexually impaired for life.'

'One assumes you didn't?' Narelle said cheekily, returning to the theatre in time to catch the tail end of the conversation. 'Helen and Peter Crowe are outside and would like to see you, Grant.'

Kate watched him go—watched them go—and once again felt a totally inappropriate niggle of what could only be described as pique.

'Watch yourself,' she warned, as she concentrated on Gareth and getting him ready for the two-hour trip to Craigtown.

'Are your weekends always this busy?' Grant asked, when, with Gareth despatched to the bigger town, they walked back to the house. 'We've barely had time to say hello, let alone go through your working hours and discuss what you want me to do.'

Katie failed to answer and, sensing her distraction, he turned to study her more closely as they walked under the light at the boundary between the house and the hospital.

'Why the frown?'

She heard him that time, spinning towards him with a hint of panic in her lovely eyes.

'Was I frowning? Did you ask something? I'm sorry.'

She pushed her hair around a bit on her head, obviously trying to remove the bits that fell forward over her face but not succeeding.

'Honestly, Grant,' she admitted, 'this motherhood thing is so weird. It's as if the body takes over from the mind in the decision-making process.'

'Not only in motherhood situations,' Grant interrupted, thinking of times, even between the two of them, when that had happened.

'I'm not talking about sex,' she snapped. 'I'm talking about everyday life, here. I mean, I should have been thinking about Gareth or whatever you were asking me but, no, my breasts are aching and I'm hoping Tara hasn't fed the baby because my body obviously thinks it's time to feed her, and I'm trying to remember when I last fed her, and if a feed's due. It's pathetic! My life is dominated by my mammary glands.'

'Not so pathetic if you think of the number of young men who failed maths as they went through Testament High, because their brains were reduced to mush by Helen Crowe's bounteous breasts. Perhaps, while you're in this situation, we could do a paper on it—the correlation between breasts and brain function from both male and female perspectives.'

They'd reached the kitchen and walked in to find Tara sitting, feet up on a chair, a book propped in front of her, while the baby slept peacefully in her arms.

'She's been fed!' Katie said, in such tragic tones Grant had to laugh.

'No, actually, she hasn't,' Tara responded. 'She had a little cry so I picked her up, changed her and carried her out to heat the milk, and by the time I got here she was asleep again.' She grinned at the pair of them and added, 'Let sleeping babies lie—isn't that the rule?'

'Most definitely,' Katie agreed, but Grant saw the way her eyes went to the sleeping infant, scanning, checking, emitting uncertainty and love in equal measure.

Not unlike what he was feeling towards Katie herself, though the love was certainly a nostalgic emotion—like an emotional hangover—inextricably linked to childhood and adolescence.

Then, because his mind seemed inclined to debate this issue, he focussed on the baby.

'Do you like Sophie as a name for her?' he asked Tara, and was pleased to see the studious young woman put down her book and earnestly consider the small face.

'Nah! She's way too pretty for a Sophie. Sophies are elegant—attractive, rather than pretty. And I reckon, though she's just about perfect now, the little scrap'll probably end up with that wild, untamed sort of look Kate has—too elemental for a Sophie.'

The statement drew protest from Katie, but Grant found himself considering it.

Elemental! That was the word he'd been looking for when he'd been thinking of Katie's fire and passion. Katie's beauty burned from within—

'I don't know where you two get off with naming my baby!'

Her protest cut into his thoughts.

'Well, you're not doing much about it,' Grant reminded her.

'I am so!' she snorted, but far too quickly for him to believe it.

'OK, tell us what you're thinking. Share a little.'

Kate saw the challenge—and amusement—in Grant's eyes, and though she longed to reel off any number of suitable names, for some reason the only female name that came immediately to mind was Hortense, and neither Grant nor Tara would believe she was seriously considering it.

She leaned over to pick up the baby, willing her to wake and demand her supper, but, of course, lacking any sense of timing—a failing she'd already lectured the baby on today—the wee thing slept on.

'My grandmother's name was Rose so I thought that might fit in somewhere,' she said, when she realised the silence in the kitchen had been caused by her failure to reply. 'Rose, Lily, Ruby, Sapphire—they're all coming back into fashion at the moment.'

Grant's expression of disbelief was so comical, she'd probably have laughed if she hadn't been feeling so confused about so many things—him being here now taking over from baby names in the prime position of concern.

'You can't call a baby any of those names,' he protested. 'Not if she's going to live in the country where people still think names like Linda are New Age. I bet Tara's mother felt very brave choosing Tara and I'm sure when Gareth's mother named him Gareth, the entire town blamed the fact that she was an in-comer—a city girl with city ways. Who was she, by the way, and what happened to her?'

'She was another teacher, and you're right about the city ways. She hated the country and left her husband with Gareth when he was only young.' Tara supplied the information then frowned at Grant.

'Why did you think of Gareth?' she demanded. 'Do you know him?'

Kate saw the flush on the girl's cheeks and remembered Gareth mentioning Tara's name. Was a romance budding between the high school's best achiever and the local bad boy?

Again?

She set aside the thought, wondering how much she could tell Tara about the accident, but before she could decide, Grant had taken over. He'd slipped into a chair opposite Tara and was explaining the accident, and when he grabbed the whiteboard Kate kept to jot down messages to herself, and began to draw a skull, Kate realised Tara was just as interested in the mechanics of the operation as she was in Gareth's well-being.

'I'll feed Hortense,' she murmured, but neither of them heard, and, as she walked through to her bedroom, she wondered if she'd have been the same—back then. Though she'd been two years behind Grant at school, and medicine hadn't always been her goal.

But the young Kate—or Katie as she had been then— and the teenage Grant accompanied her, like friendly ghosts, to the bedroom, and, as the baby began to suckle and her stomach muscles tightened in response, she couldn't help but think of that other summer.

'Coming swimming, Katie?' he'd asked, and his voice, so familiar though he'd only started phoning her regularly since the holidays had begun, had made her stomach cramp and tighten, while her heart had flip-flopped in her chest like a just-landed fish.

'I'll have to ask Mum,' she'd said, knowing she'd tell her mother it was Sally on the phone. Her mother wouldn't have stopped her seeing Grant—it was just that the shift in their relationship had been too new, too delicate and fragile, to be shared.

'It's OK. I'll ride out,' she'd said, returning to the phone once the lie had been accepted and permission given.

'See you soon,' he'd said, and she'd known he'd ride to meet her, then they'd turn off near the boundary to his parents' property, seeking a secluded stretch of the river where the banks were steep so the cattle rarely strayed.

'It wasn't that the cattle were a problem,' Kate told the baby. 'Only the people who might be looking for them and inadvertently find us.'

Not that they'd planned to go beyond the kissing—not that day, or really any other day in the near future.

'The kissing was mind-blowing enough,' Kate said, burping the baby before shifting her to the other side. 'The shift from friends to more than friends was really weird. It just happened those holidays and, boy, did it happen. Talk about passion!'

The memory brought a warmth she hadn't felt for ages, but the baby had fallen asleep and needed to be changed again before she was settled for the night—or whatever part of it she might happen to sleep.

'It must have been the heat—or only having swimsuits on,' she told the sleeping infant, while her body, so long dormant, now rippled with sensations that had nothing to do with breastfeeding.

A tap on the door made her look up, feeling so guilty about her thoughts she could feel her cheeks awash with heated colour.

'Tara's just gone. I walked her home, but I didn't pay her. Should I have done?'

'No!' Kate said, then realised the word had sounded far too abrupt when Grant put up his hands as if to ward off an attack.

'Hey, I was only asking about paying the babysitter, not if I could mount an assault on your virtue.'

Kate shook her head, then she gave a quiet laugh.

'Actually,' she admitted, 'that's more or less what I was saying no to. I was thinking about that last summer—about the day you rang to ask me to go swimming.'

Grant was startled by the admission, but the funny little smile lingering around Katie's lips, and the softness in her voice, suggested the memories were happy ones.

'We did enjoy it, didn't we?' she said, busying herself with changing the baby's nappy so he could no longer see her face. 'I mean, it *was* fun, wasn't it? Not just a rose-coloured-glasses view of the past.'

Uncertain how to respond, but aware of a need to step with the greatest delicacy, Grant walked closer, then, as she finished wrapping the baby in the snug cotton sheet, he lifted the little bundle and held her to his shoulder.

'It was the best summer of my life,' he said simply. 'Not just because I discovered sex, but because I discovered it with you.'

This time Katie's look was of blank astonishment.

'You discovered sex with me? But you'd had... Everyone said... You made out...'

The run of unfinished sentences ended abruptly and she came closer, peering up into his face.

'Are you telling me, Grant Bell, that you knew no more about it than I did? That we were both virgins?'

He nodded, though not sure it was the correct thing to do right now.

'Well, of all the cheek!' she stormed. Remembering the baby, Katie seized her from Grant's arms, tucked her back into the crib, then all but shoved him out of the room, shutting the door behind them, no doubt so she could yell without waking the baby.

'You let me believe you knew all about it. You even told me the proper names for bits of my anatomy I'd barely realised existed, and gave me a lecture on what happens during orgasm. Were you making it all up?'

Grant hustled her towards the kitchen.

'I'd read it out of a book Mum had at home,' he admitted. 'She'd bought it for my sisters to read.'

'But you had condoms!' Kate reminded him.

'Everyone had condoms—well, all males of teenage years had them, and I wouldn't be surprised if some of the girls didn't carry them as well!' Grant replied. 'Talk about hopeful! I'd actually had a supply of them since I was twelve. Every time we went to Craigtown, I'd get a packet at the supermarket. And don't look so shocked—it was better than buying them at Patterson's Pharmacy here in Testament. Mrs P. would have been on the phone to Mum before I was out the door.'

Kate shook her head, though somewhere, deep inside, was a little bubble of warmth she suspected might have been generated by pleasure at Grant's revelations.

Though he needn't know that.

Definitely needn't know that...

'I can't believe you made out—' she began, but he interrupted with his wide-eyed, innocent 'who, me?' look, followed by a smile of sheer devilment.

'Actually,' he said softly, 'we both "made out"—remember?'

She was twenty-eight years of age, a doctor and a mother, and she was *not* going to blush!

But just in case, she turned away.

'That isn't what I meant, and you know it,' she muttered, heading back to the kitchen for a cup of tea before going to bed. 'I can't believe you pretended to know it all! Or pretended to know, in the biblical sense, most of the girls in town.'

'Would it have made any difference?'

She had to turn again, to face him, and when she realised he was serious, she had to think about it.

'I would probably have been far more tentative and uncertain, but I was such a show-off that thinking *you* knew it all made me anxious not to appear a complete amateur.'

She shook her head, remembering.

'Gosh, we were intense, weren't we? I don't think I've ever felt that level of intensity in a relationship since then. It was probably a hormonal thing, like risk-taking among teenagers. Once the hormones settle down, you don't get that terrible rush of heat and longing.'

She spoke with clinical detachment, as if it was something that had happened to two other people. So why, Grant wondered, did his body feel a faint quickening of interest?

Because whatever he'd had with Katie was unfinished?

Because 'that terrible rush of heat and longing' described those feelings so well, and he, too, had never experienced them again.

'What *are* you thinking about?' she demanded. 'Do you want a cup of tea is one of those "answer yes or no" type questions. It doesn't require frowns, or even a great deal of brain power to reply.'

He looked into the green eyes and told himself it was dangerous to think of anything apart from the job. Excessively dangerous to go wallowing into the murky waters of the past. Worse than diving into unexplored parts of the creek—near where they'd...

'Sorry, didn't hear you. Yes, please.'

'I've shop biscuits. They may be a bit old, but I've a wonderful assortment of jam, pickles and chutneys to spread on them to disguise the oldness. I think everyone in town has brought me a bottle of homemade something since I've been here. They've been good that way. There are the hard scones as well.'

She was bustling around the kitchen, filling the electric kettle and setting it to boil, finding mugs, tea bags, talking.

Talking?

Grant smiled to himself.

Katie had always talked too much when she was nervous. Maybe the nostalgic memories had quickened *her* body, too.

So he needn't feel so bad, and he could put the small incident behind him, back in the furthest pigeonholes of his mind where those happy teenage memories belonged.

'There!' She set a mug on the table in front of him, with the air of someone who'd just split the atom using only a blunt kitchen knife. 'I've sugar somewhere if you want it, and litres and litres of milk. You want milk?'

Grant picked up the string of the tea bag and jiggled it furiously, hoping to darken the watery brew.

'No milk, no sugar. Working in A and E makes shopping erratic so, rather than hating the taste of tea with no milk when it went sour or with no sugar when I ran out, I learned to live without both.'

'Why A and E?' she asked, dropping into a chair opposite him, removing her tea bag and placing it on a saucer.

Grant hesitated, then decided there was nothing to be gained by not telling the truth.

'Money,' he said simply, then he grinned at the astonishment in her eyes.

'Hey, I had my reasons,' he said, hoping to banish the disbelief which had followed the astonishment. For some unknown reason, he didn't want Katie thinking badly of him. 'When we had to leave the property—and I know it wasn't your father's fault, no matter how I acted at the time—we shifted to Sydney where Mum's family were. But the country was still in my blood and I vowed I'd get the place back one day. Well, maybe not that property but *a* property. Somewhere I could run a few cattle—I didn't want the hassle of sheep or even crops.'

He shrugged, then smiled as he admitted, 'I guess it was that teenage intensity you were talking about earlier. Anyway, you'd always talked about becoming a doctor, and I knew a lot of doctors made a lot of money so, once I'd accepted I wasn't going to be raising cattle in the immediate future, I thought I'd be a doctor, earn heaps and buy back the farm.'

'Easy-peasy!' Katie teased.

'Exactly,' Grant agreed, though the silly phrase jolted his complacency about having the past tucked securely back in the pigeonholes. 'Once I qualified, I stayed in hospitals, working the weekend and night shifts in A and E whenever possible, often moonlighting as well in private twenty-four-hour clinics or on-call services.'

'And when did you realise you'd kill yourself with work before you ever had enough money to buy a cattle property around here?'

Her lips flickered into a smile, her eyes were alight with a teasing laughter and he found himself grinning happily back at her, feeling dangerously at home in Katie's house—in Katie's life!

More than at home...

'Pretty soon after I'd started,' he admitted, banishing all other thoughts. 'I decided I could settle for somewhere less expensive, fewer cattle, maybe a hobby farm. Though, by the time I figured it out, I was hooked on the A and E department. Talk about an adrenalin junkie! I'd have fitted right into one of those manic scenes in televised medical dramas.'

'So you stayed three years?'

He nodded, but realised just how close he'd come to talking about other things.

'Well, it's been a long day. I might head for bed. OK if I use the bathroom?'

Kate nodded, and watched him leave the room. They hadn't discussed work tomorrow, or wages, or shared housekeeping, or any of the things which should have been discussed, but when she'd asked about the length of his stay in A and E, a dark shadow had clouded Grant's blue eyes and drawn lines of strain down his cheeks, and she'd known he needed to get away.

Right then!

Before he told her more?

What kind of more?

She shivered in the warm night air, sensing a darkness in the heart and soul of her old childhood companion—some kind of wound that hadn't healed. And her heart, which she'd been sure was armour-plated against all emotion, ached for Grant.

CHAPTER FIVE

GRANT BELL was the last person on her mind as Kate stumbled into the kitchen in the light of early dawn. The baby—today, much later today, she'd decide on a name—had woken every two hours, and though she'd gone happily back to sleep after each feed, for a new mother hoping to get four or even six hours' straight sleep, the two-hourly demands had been a nightmare.

Kate poured milk into a mug and, clutching it in one hand and a slice of bread in the other, was making her way back to bed, fuzzily working out that if she went straight to sleep now, and could stay asleep until eight, she'd have—five from eight leaves three—three hours' sleep before starting work at eight-fifteen. Surely she could shower and dress in ten—

'Go back to bed and stay there!' The gruff order interrupted her muddled mathematical calculations. 'I'll take the morning surgery—it's why I'm here after all. If I need any help Vi can't give or information she can't supply, I'll phone you.'

Kate stared blankly at the man who'd emerged from the spare bedroom. She'd known he was there—had been aware, all through the night, of another presence in the house. But seeing him, recognising him as Grant, standing and talking to him—she in a faded old shirt she wore to bed, and he in boxer shorts that seemed, to her sleep-deprived eyes, to have big red lips all over them—was too way out to believe.

'I thought I might have dreamt you,' she admitted, then added ruefully, 'Though I guess I'd have to have been asleep to dream, wouldn't I?'

'Bad night?'

'Just interrupted,' Kate said quickly, remembering she'd promised herself she wouldn't be one of those mothers who complained all the time about the demands of any aspect of motherhood.

'Though they've every right to complain about two-hourly night feeds!' she grumbled to herself.

Then she glanced guiltily at Grant, hoping he hadn't heard. But if he had, he gave no sign of it, merely studying her with an intent kind of interest, as if he, too, was slightly bemused to find the two of them meeting like this in a passageway.

'Bed!' he repeated, making a command of the word, and Kate's mind, fuzzy with tiredness, wondered how it would sound as an invitation.

'And don't smile at me like that!' he added, sounding quite cross now, so she didn't dare to ask, Like what? 'I'll do morning surgery, you rest. We can talk over lunch, decide on a rough programme, then shop before afternoon surgery.'

'That sounds suspiciously like a list,' Kate told him.

'It's not a list, it's a plan. Now go back to bed, Katie, before Fiona wakes again.'

'Fiona? I thought you'd decided on Sophie—for this week at least.'

'I'm flexible,' Grant said with a grin, then he put his hand on her shoulder, turned her around and steered her into her bedroom.

Which was when Kate realised just how great a danger to her peace of mind Grant Bell represented.

It wasn't so much the touch, which had started the shivery-skin phenomenon again, as the rightness of the touch—and *that* was a really scary thought!

She glanced over to where he was studying the sleeping baby, trying out the name Fiona, if Kate's reading of his lips was correct. Tall, lean and hard, though she doubted he did much physical work these days, there was a familiarity about Grant as if the very cells that made up her body recognised a match in his.

Nonsensical meanderings of an overtired mind, Kate chided herself, but her eyes continued to watch him, and her body cells to recognise his.

Well, she hoped that's all it was—the recognition thing—because there was no way she could possibly be feeling sexy. Not two weeks after giving birth—it just wasn't possible. And Grant Bell was passing through Testament, then going back to his Linda, while she was setting up a life for herself and the baby—a life and a career.

'I think Fiona would suit her.'

The statement startled Kate, bringing her abruptly out of her straying thoughts, but not swiftly enough to deny his words.

'I'll think about it,' she said, 'when I've had some sleep and my brain starts functioning again.'

She smiled at Grant, because he was there, and being kind, and it certainly wasn't his fault her body was behaving the way it was.

'I'm glad you're here,' she admitted.

He'd been doing all right until she'd smiled, Grant realised as he left the room, shutting the door firmly on the woman and sleeping baby. Or had it been the 'I'm glad you're here' that had thrown him?

Whatever—but the two, taken in conjunction, had caused a tremor that could only be anxiety. And given his decision to remain preferably single and definitely childless, getting tremors of any kind in a bedroom with a sensual woman and tiny sleeping baby was not good.

But she had looked so incredibly sexy, in her big, loose shirt, her hair tousled into a tangle so seductively sensual it was all he could do to keep his hands out of it. Maybe it was because she was feeding the baby, and positively oozing maternal hormones, that his body found her disturbingly attractive. It was all to do with primal urges, and procreation, with a bit of a protection thing thrown in. Though he, of all people, knew protection didn't extend far—knew the futility of thinking anyone could keep another human being safe.

He went through to the kitchen, his arms aching again in a way they hadn't ached for eighteen months, and, as he slumped into a chair and stared out the window at the pale relentless blue of an early summer morning sky, he wondered why he'd come to Testament.

And why he hadn't realised his coming would peel away the scabs of healing wounds and expose him to pain he'd thought he'd conquered.

'You came because Vi said Katie needed help, and helping anyone was better than hanging around a beach that lacked enough swell to make a ripple, let alone a wave, feeling sorry for yourself,' he reminded himself. 'And speaking of Vi, it's time you got dressed and went over to investigate the surgery. No! Bakery first. Some fresh bread. Maybe Katie would like a pastry or two when she wakes later.'

Which was being practical, not protective.

Thus assured his motives were OK, he was out the door and almost at the back lane when he realised he was wearing the 'hot lips' boxer shorts and nothing else. Shirtless might just pass in Testament at six in the morning, but boxer shorts?

He doubted it!

Back inside he pulled board shorts over the boxers and a flowered shirt over his chest. Looking at the flowers reminded him of the fictitious Chlorinda. He'd invented her on the spur of the moment, to make it easier for Katie to accept him, then hadn't followed up on the idea. Should he let that story drop completely, keep her in reserve, or bring her to the fore of his conversation—use her like a shield to deflect the emotional weakness he was in danger of exposing if he became too involved in Katie's and Fiona's lives?

It was a dilemma he would normally have considered as he walked briskly down the road towards the shops, but a carolling magpie peering, bright-eyed, down at him from the branch of a she-oak, raucously chattering galahs flying like a pink cloud overhead, the scent of eucalypts in the air, the sun flirting with the leaves, turning them from green to silver, all combined to banish thought from his mind. He moved along, barely conscious of the physical effort as his body revelled in a sense of homecoming so strong he wanted to shout out loud and spread his arms wide enough to embrace the world.

'Embrace the bloody world? You've gone bonkers, you have!' he muttered, then he nodded good morning to a startled dog walker who'd caught him talking to himself.

He concentrated on practical matters—food first, then check out the appointment book in the surgery and have a quick look at the patient files so he wouldn't be completely at a loss when the patients came in. Too late now to phone Vi to assure her he'd arrived safely but, given the efficiency of country-town grapevines, she'd probably know anyway.

'Grant Bell! Heard you were back in town but didn't believe it.'

The greeting, as he walked into the bakery, redolent with the smell of new-baked bread, suggested the grapevine still worked, but though the face which uttered it was familiar it took a while to dredge up a name.

'Codger? Codger Williams? But your father was the postmaster, not the baker.'

Codger—whose real name, Grant remembered now, had been Bill, William Williams of all things—shoved out a hand the size of a baseball glove.

'Never fancied eating letters,' he said. 'Did my apprenticeship here under old Harry Smart and took over when he retired. Not that he properly retired—the old fellow still comes in each day to tell me what I've done wrong with the pies or coffee rolls.'

Grant shook the offered hand and, suspecting Codger was about to embark on a lengthy game of 'do you remember', gave his order.

'I'll be back to have a chat as soon as I'm settled,' he said. 'But since arriving yesterday I've been on the run so I haven't had time to check out the surgery.'

'Fancy you becoming a doctor,' Codger said, using tongs to lift pastries into a white paper bag. 'Katie Fenton—well, we all knew she'd go that way. Bloody brilliant, she was. But bad boy Bell? That's a different story. Saw the light, did you? Decided there was more money to be made in the medical profession than swiping chocolates off the display in the newsagent's?'

'Ben Whiting swiped the chocolates, I just got the blame,' Grant protested, though his mind was scooting backwards, wondering if everyone in town—including all the patients he was about to see—would have a 'bad boy Bell' tale to tell.

'Yeah?' Codger said, making the word so disbelieving Grant knew it would be a waste of breath to argue.

He handed over a note, and took the change and his purchases, leaving the shop with a promise to return to talk over old times.

Not in this lifetime! he added to himself as he walked back towards the house. As if I don't have enough embarrassing memories of my own without people like Codger digging up more.

The walk back to the house was undertaken with a marked diminution of enthusiasm. So much so, the thought of the wave-less beach seemed positively enticing. He tried reminding himself it was nearly Christmas, but it was so long since he'd felt anything approaching a festive spirit at this time of the year that the thought was more dampening than uplifting.

But when he moved quietly through to the bedrooms, opening Katie's door and peering in, the sight of her, sleeping deeply, as if confident he'd take care of everything, reminded him that it was good to be needed sometimes.

He glanced towards the crib and saw the baby stirring, then, before he could decide if picking her up would be a good idea, she gave a funny snuffle, made a little grunting noise and waved her arms as if expecting company. Telling himself it was just this once, and picking her up didn't mean getting involved, he crossed the room in two long strides and lifted her, turning to snag a couple of everything from the piles of baby necessities by the bed.

He saw the sling, hooked over the doorknob, as he was leaving the room, and grabbed that as well.

'I know there's expressed milk in the fridge, but as it doesn't come with a use-by date, I have no idea if it's fresh. No idea how long it stays fresh, now I come to think of it. Debbie used formula. But as I also know you were fed only an hour ago, I think we'll give it a miss.'

The huge blue eyes studied him, as if taking in every word he said, remaining fixed on his face as he set her down on the couch and proceeded with nappy changing.

'I'm quite adept at this,' he told her. 'Which is good for you, as I might be doing a bit of it over the next few weeks. Your mother needs to rest. You understand that, don't you?'

The sling took longer to work out than he'd expected, but eventually he had the baby tied securely, if not neatly, to the front of his chest.

'Damn! Should have had the cup of tea first so I don't run the risk of slopping scalding liquid over your downy head.'

He peered down at the downy head in question, and added, 'Though now you appear to have gone back to sleep, that's less likely to happen.'

Moving cautiously as he adjusted to the difference in his

body shape, he set out the pastries on a plate and covered them with plastic film so Katie would see them when she came into the kitchen. Made himself toast, and decided to risk the tea, though he did add cold water so, should an accident occur, it would be warm and not scalding liquid splashing everywhere, concentrating all the time on the practical, so he didn't have to think about the warm bundle pressed against his chest.

'Good heavens, look at Dr Dad!'

He swung from the sink where he was rinsing off his plate to see Aunt Vi come through the door. He moved towards her, leaning carefully forward far enough to plant a big kiss on his favourite relative's cheek.

'Katie's sleeping and Fiona didn't need feeding, so I thought I'd keep her occupied for a while,' he explained.

'Fiona? Kate's finally named her, then?'

Vi seemed so pleased Grant hated to disabuse her of the notion, but honesty compelled him to explain.

'You can't try out names on babies!' his relative protested.

'Why not?' he demanded. 'It seems eminently sensible to me. Anyway, I should be over at the surgery learning what's where, not arguing with you about a name for a baby that doesn't belong to either of us.'

Vi cast him a funny look.

'Bringing too much back, is it? I did wonder when I asked you to come, but after that wretched Paul left town, then the locum woman let Kate down so badly, I had to find someone.'

'I was happy to come,' Grant assured her. He couldn't bring himself to deny the 'bringing too much back' comment, so he let it slide. 'Now, did you want something from here, or were you just checking there was a doctor available to start work?'

'I was just checking,' Vi said, 'but now I've checked, are you really coming to work like that?'

Grant peered downward.

'I thought I'd take the baby off before I start. Katie said you'd been minding her at work.'

'I wasn't talking about the baby, but the shirt,' Vi told him. 'And the shorts.'

'It's all I have. No, I lie! I have one pair of long, cotton, draw-string trousers—cargo pants really—but it's far too hot for long pants out here. They were for going out. I've been in Byron Bay, remember.'

'Yes!' Vi said faintly, then she squared her shoulders as if readying herself for battle. 'Well, if a single, pregnant Katie Fenton arriving in town as the new doctor shocked a bit of life into the place, I can't wait to see what you in your lurid beach gear is going to do!'

'Liven the locals up a little more,' Grant said, smiling and moving closer to give his aunt a hug.

She responded with a quick kiss on his cheek.

'It's about time you came home,' she said.

Home?

Now, that was a scary—no, forget scary, that was a positively terrifying thought.

An impossible thought.

'I've only come to help Katie out,' he reminded Vi. 'And seeing how isolated she is, I'm glad I was available. You know that hospital doctor did nothing more than the basic checks during her pregnancy, and there are no antenatal classes. The poor woman's been at her wit's end.'

'She told you all of that?' Vi demanded.

Grant peered at his aunt, puzzled by the disbelief in her voice.

'Why shouldn't she?'

'Why shouldn't she?' Vi repeated. 'There's no earthly reason why she shouldn't except that, since the moment she arrived in town, she's been Miss Independent. Miss I-can-manage-on-my-own. Offers of help were met with polite smiles and thanks but, no, thanks. I was surprised when

I took a casserole around and she didn't give it straight back to me.'

The picture Vi was painting was disturbing, and as his aunt pulled patient files from the shelves, and he unwound Fiona from his chest, he said, speaking more to himself than to Vi, 'I wonder why? I wonder what made her so unwilling to accept favours from people? Even to the extent of assuring her parents she didn't need them here for the baby's birth?'

'From what I can gather, both the baby's father and her own mother suggested an abortion,' Vi said, closing the cupboard door and turning to take the baby from his arms. 'So perhaps she feels, having decided to go it alone, she doesn't deserve help, particularly from strangers—which is what we are to her after all these years.'

'That's why her parents should be here—or at least her mother. Katie says they'd planned their overseas trip for years, but I wonder if there's more to it. If there's been a family feud over her keeping the baby.'

Vi led the way to the reception area, then turned towards him.

'She was always a bit of a snob, Mrs Fenton,' she mused. 'And since he became State Manager of the bank, I imagine she's got worse. Kate's choice of single motherhood mightn't have sat well with her. But Kate was always a loyal young thing—she certainly wouldn't say if there'd been serious trouble.'

'You're right about the loyalty, but there can't be an irreparable feud. She sent Katie recipes.'

'Which the poor girl needed like a hole in the head,' Vi fumed. 'Overseas trip or not, Mrs Fenton should have come herself. She should be cooking not only all the meals but stocking up the freezer for when she leaves, and babysitting while Kate works, and taking her granddaughter for walks, and generally supporting her daughter, not sending flaming recipes.'

Grant smiled at Vi's vehemence.

'If the scones were an example of the way Katie cooks, they probably will be flaming,' he said. 'But enough of Katie for now. Let's see the patient list. Who do I know?'

'Just about everyone, though they've all aged a bit.' Vi set the baby down in a little basket positioned on a wide table at the back of the reception area. Beside it, neatly stacked, were piles of baby gear, similar to the ones in Katie's bedroom.

'Does no one use cupboards and little chests of drawers any more?' he asked, forgetting they were supposed to be in work-mode.

'That's another thing her mother should have seen to,' Vi said darkly. 'The poor girl has no baby furniture and changing that baby on the bed instead of on a high table or baby-changing thingy will wreck her back.'

Grant tucked the words 'baby furniture' into the back of his mind, though he could see it all—the chest of drawers with duckling decals on it, the changing table with little pockets everywhere for the odds and ends a baby needed, the bag that hung from the ceiling and held folded nappies.

'You'd better remind me who people are,' he said to Vi, shoving the mental image back into the furthermost corner of his mind. 'You know, the old "you remember Mrs Woulfe" trick.'

'I'll try,' Vi told him, 'though there are sure to be some slip-ups. It's twelve years since you were in town, and we have had some newcomers in that time.'

'A new bank manager for a start,' Grant said, reading through the names in the appointment book and trying to put faces to them. 'How long ago did the Fentons leave?'

'When Katie was in her final year of high school. They actually left mid-year and she stayed on with the Williams family so she didn't have to move schools.'

'Codger Williams's family?'

'That's right,' Vi replied, totally unconcerned by this

revelation that was causing Grant considerable dismay, though why he wasn't sure. Actually, he was sure! The thought of the teenage Katie and the libidinous Codger sharing a bathroom was enough to make anyone uneasy, no matter how far in the past it was.

He concentrated on the names.

'Mrs Russell—that's not old Mrs Russell, is it? She was over a hundred before we left town.'

'She was eighty-eight when you left town and turned a hundred earlier this year. Her kidneys are giving up and the specialist down in Brisbane recommended she go on this Eprex. It means weekly injections. Kate got a lot of information about it, and has to order in the injections through the specialist. I'll get the file.'

She passed a thick file to Grant, who opened it and found the information leaflets explaining the drug Mrs Russell would be getting. Eprex was a trade name for erythropoietin, a hormone synthesised in the kidneys and released into the blood to stimulate the production of red blood cells.

In people with chronic renal disease, the kidneys failed to produce the hormone, leading to a drop in the red blood cells. Because these cells carried oxygen throughout the body, the patient suffered from breathlessness and the general debility a lack of oxygen would cause. But athletes, needing an increased oxygen-carrying capacity to give them an added edge, would find the hormone invaluable. No doubt it was on the banned list, which explained why only specialists could prescribe it.

He read through the rest of the information, then the most recent pages of Mrs Russell's file. Though he'd seen cases of acute renal failure during his years in A and E, he'd usually slated such patients for admission and passed the problem on to people better trained to deal with the disease.

Vi tapped on the door and helped Mrs Russell manoeuvre her wheelie-walker into the room.

'You remember Mrs Russell,' Vi said, following orders but totally unnecessarily in this case. 'Granny, this is Grant Bell. My nephew. He's doing Kate's job for a while.'

'So bad boy Bell's come back, has he?' Granny Russell cackled, and Grant, who'd been thinking country GP work might be more interesting than he'd thought, groaned inwardly and wondered how long it would be before the locals dropped the 'bad boy' tag.

Speaking slowly and carefully, he led Granny through a recital of her general health—bowel and bladder habits, fluid intake and appetite—while taking her blood pressure, a surprisingly reasonable one hundred and sixty over seventy, pulse and checking her lungs for any sign of congestion.

'I'm good as I was at eighty,' she told him. 'Maybe even better, since Kate sent me to Brisbane to get my kidneys checked and we started on these injections. You know, some of the lads in the high school football team'd kill to have some of the stuff I get.'

'You're right there, Granny,' Grant told her, surprised to find the old woman knew so much about the drug—and obviously had no trouble remembering what she'd been told about it. 'Nothing much wrong with your memory, is there?' he said, wondering why some people retained all their mental faculties while others began losing theirs so early.

'Nothing wrong with most of me—just my kidneys,' Granny said. 'The specialist said I was too old for a transplant, though I bet they've given them to people who didn't appreciate a second chance as much as I would.'

She was so definite that Grant was startled into questioning the remark.

'What would you do with a second chance, Granny?'

She looked up at him, the rheumy blue eyes as alert as those of the magpie he'd passed earlier.

'Live a little, love a little,' she sang, so off-key both she and Grant started laughing, though when she started coughing she sobered up and said, 'We all deserve a second chance, don't you think?'

'I do,' Grant agreed, though he wasn't so sure it covered both the suggestions she'd made. 'And that being the case, how about you start with me? Spread the word I'm a nice guy—no longer bad boy Bell.'

Granny laughed again, then told him to get away with him.

'You were never really bad, just into everything,' she said. 'The name kind of suited you.'

She eyed his clothes as he unwrapped the syringe.

'I should get a shirt like that,' she said.

'I'm glad you like it,' Grant said. 'Aunt Vi was horrified, but I *was* on holiday at the beach when she phoned and asked me to come. Now, where do you want this? Upper arm, thigh, stomach? Any preference?'

'Kate did the right thigh last time, so let's go for upper arm. My left one, as I've got a lot of cooking to do this afternoon.'

She studied Grant for a minute.

'If I gave you some cookies you'd take them, wouldn't you?'

He nodded, and she smiled and bared her arm, ready for him to swab it then inject the drug just under the skin.

He was seeing his elderly patient out when the phone rang. Knowing it was likely to be Katie, waking to find her baby had been stolen, he hovered by the reception desk so he could hear at least one end of the conversation.

'No, she's fine. She's sleeping. I'll bring her over when she wakes. In the meantime, as Grant hasn't killed his first patient, why don't you relax and enjoy a morning off?'

Grant smiled as he imagined Katie's reaction, but Vi would have none of it.

'Don't you come near this surgery!' she ordered. 'I've already told you I'll bring Fiona over when she wakes.'

Grant could hear Katie's protests from four feet away.

'Oh, sorry!' Vi said. 'It must be the excitement of seeing him again. I was sure he said you'd decided.'

There was a pause then Vi added, 'Sophie yesterday? Well, I like Sophie. Mind you, I like Fiona, too.'

The look of shock on Vi's face suggested Katie had slammed the receiver down in her ear.

Suspecting she'd come barrelling over to give him a piece of her mind, he grabbed the next file, checked the name, looked enquiringly at Vi who shook her head just enough to tell him he didn't know the patient, then he called Mr Ridley in.

'Brian Ridley,' the man said, when Grant had closed the door and introduced himself. 'I'm the bank manager, though I didn't take over from Dr Fenton's father. There were three or four in between him and me.'

The man seemed nervous but, then, patients often were. With reason, considering some of the things they were expected to tell their doctors.

'How can I help you?' Grant asked, and Brian looked around the room, his eyes darting desperately from one poster to the next, as if seeking some solution to whatever ailed him.

They settled on a warning that immunisation didn't last for ever, the thrust of it being one should have regular boosters, especially for tetanus.

'I haven't had a t-tetanus needle f-for a while,' Brian stammered, and Grant, wise in the way of patient denial, wondered just how serious the real problem was.

'Are you planning some digging in the garden? Or are you around horses a lot?'

The man looked startled.

'No. Why? Are regular tetanus shots only recommended for people who will be in contact with horses? Can't ordinary people get them as a precautionary measure? Doesn't tetanus lead to lockjaw? That would be a terrible thing to get.'

Especially for a bank manager, Grant thought but didn't say.

'I'm only filling in here,' he said aloud, 'so I'm not certain what's kept on the premises. I'll check with Vi if we've tetanus vaccine available. If not, I'll write you a script, you can pick it up at the chemist and come back for the shot.'

'Are you doing all the surgery sessions?' he asked, and Grant, thinking maybe Brian would be able to pluck up the courage to talk about what really was wrong, said reassuringly, 'Yes! Just for a week or so until Katie gets back on her feet.'

'She doesn't like being called Katie,' Brian said earnestly, but it was the pink that washed into his ears at the same time that gave him away.

'Yes, unfortunately,' Vi said later, when Grant, after inoculating Brian against tetanus and sending him on his way, relayed his suspicions to her. 'The poor man is hopelessly, besottedly, helplessly in love with Kate and she's the only person in town who doesn't know it. She says he's being nice to her because she's part of the bank family. Honestly, he moons around the place, mows her lawn on Saturdays, comes in for appointments on the flimsiest of pretences, rushes out to serve her when she goes into the bank, and she all but pats him on the head, like you would a favoured pet.'

'I hope he isn't married—making an idiot of himself like that!' Grant muttered, failing to see the amusement that was shaking Vi's frame.

'No, he's a bachelor. It makes it even funnier because he's been in town three years now, and every unwed woman within kilometres—and a few married ones as well, no doubt—have made a play for him. We'd all begun to think he was gay when Kate arrives in town and, bang, Brian falls for her in a big way!'

Grant frowned at his still chortling aunt.

'Isn't that baby awake? Shouldn't you be taking her back to her mother?'

He grabbed the next file, read out the name, and it wasn't until he was heading back to the consulting room, the patient, Mrs Milward, on his heels, that he realised here was someone else he knew.

He swung around.

'Mrs Milward who taught me in Grade Two?'

The woman beamed at him.

'Fancy you remembering that! Though you always were a clever boy.'

'But you left town,' he said, remembering the big party at the school when he'd been a few years older.

'I came back,' she said simply. 'When you find a place as nice as Testament, you know you have to come back.'

Yeah, well! Grant thought, then he shoved the words way back in his mind, with the nursery furniture and second chances. Right now he had to concentrate on work.

CHAPTER SIX

KATE, feeling alive and well after the extra sleep and a long, hot shower, where she'd had time to wash her hair, met Vi halfway between the house and the surgery and took the baby from her, peering down into her daughter's face as if to check she had the right child.

'I don't think she looks much like a Fiona, do you?' she said, inviting Vi to join her in her scrutiny.

'You can't tell at that age,' Vi said firmly. 'But you can't call her Fiona Fenton anyway. Too many "f"s".'

'You're right. Will you tell Grant or should I?' She heard the stupidity of the question and immediately repudiated it. 'No, that's nonsense. So's this name-practising he's carrying on with. I'll just ignore him.'

And on that eminently sensible note she headed for the house, where, as the baby—she wondered if Sophie would do—looked as if she might sleep for ever, Kate put her back in her crib and did some housework, finding pleasure in simple household tasks she rarely found time to do.

Once dusting, vacuuming and dishwashing were finished, she went back into the garden and picked some long strands of gaudy pink and white bougainvillaea, bringing them inside and filling three vases with the bright blooms. The house looked like a home again.

'Which is what we need, sweet thing,' she told the baby, who finally woke and demanded feeding now—immediately! 'A home. Our home. Yours and mine.'

'It must have been the sleep,' she explained to Grant a little later, when he'd walked back to the house after surgery to find a salad lunch and crisp rolls awaiting him. 'I woke up so full of energy I not only cleaned the house but, after the baby was fed, we shopped as well. I know you wanted to be part of that expedition, so I left the butcher for you.'

Grant seemed puzzled—well, he seemed more stunned but as she hadn't done anything to actually stun him, after all everyone shopped—she went with puzzled.

'Mick Gazecki works there,' she explained, thinking maybe it was the butcher part puzzling him. 'He was in my year, but you'd probably remember him. Worst flirt in the world. He's married now with about five little Gazeckis and even when I was hugely pregnant and ugly as sin with it, he carried on with the kind of winks and comments that made me want to hit him with his meat cleaver.'

'Do you still have these murderous urges or was it part of being pregnant? Like cravings?'

Kate considered the question for a moment. 'I don't think it was a pregnancy thing—I didn't get cravings either.' She grinned at him. 'So you'll just have to take your chances, won't you? But I don't have a meat cleaver, only a very blunt knife.'

'That's reassuring,' Grant said, though in truth he was less reassured—less assured as well—than he made out. He'd wandered back over to the house filled with a kind of low-key anticipation commensurate with sharing work talk with a colleague.

Then he'd seen the colleague and been struck dumb. The transformation was surely more than a few hours' sleep could have achieved. There had to be a fairy godmother, complete with magic wand, lurking in the background.

Katie shone! From the top of her freshly washed head, ablaze with golden curls, to the tips of her freshly painted toenails, she gleamed with such radiant well-being he felt dull and lifeless just looking at her.

Though there was little dull or lifeless about his physical reaction. No, sir!

However, with the discussion centring on meat cleavers,

now wasn't the time to be admitting to any physical reactions.

'You were supposed to be sleeping, not tidying the house or shopping.'

He was aware he sounded cross, but couldn't help it. Not that it affected her at all. She simply beamed at him and held out her arms as if for inspection.

'I did sleep,' she said, 'then I washed my hair and shaved my legs...' she raised a ridiculously long, tanned leg for him to inspect '...and cleaned the house and picked flowers and fed the baby and still had time to shop.'

'In those shorts?' The words were out before he could stop them, and Katie's startled look, followed by a slight narrowing of emerald green eyes, told him exactly what she thought of the question.

'And who are you to question what I wear? The fashion police?' She pointed derisively at his shirt. 'The final arbiter in suitable man-about-the-country attire?'

Seething with the injustice of her words, and with her ingratitude and attitude and attractive legs, Grant scowled at her.

'I was thinking it's no wonder the local butcher leers at you!' he said, then he saw her lower lip and remembered how Katie had always hidden any uncertainty or pain behind a show of bravado—the showier the better.

'Oh, Katie, don't cry. I didn't mean it.' Two strides took him around the table so he could put his arm around her and draw her lush softness close to his body.

She blinked away the tears, and the smile this time was soft and very genuine.

'I really don't want to cry,' she said. 'I mean, I'm not unhappy. I think there might be a link between milk ducts and tear ducts which would explain why nursing women become weepy at the slightest provocation.'

She wriggled out of his embrace, which, given his body's

reaction and her attitude to Mick Gazecki and meat cleavers, was a good idea.

'Let's eat,' she suggested. 'And you can tell me all about your morning. Did Granny Russell come in? And who remembered you?'

Grant returned to the opposite side of the table and sat down.

'Everyone remembered me—well, not so much remembered me as remembered bad boy Bell. If I'd heard those words once more, I swear I'd have belted whoever said them.'

'You might have to borrow Mick's meat cleaver!' she teased, as Grant tackled his salad with enthusiasm. Sublimating one hunger with another? 'Though I'm sure they think of bad boy Bell with affection, whereas their Katie Fenton memories are recalled with shock and much tut-tutting. I imagine my return, pregnant and unmarried, led to a spate of "I told you she'd come to no good!" comments among the locals.'

'But you'd have known that before you came—you'd lived in country towns long enough to know how they operate.'

She had her head down, slicing soft pink ham and pushing it onto her fork, so he couldn't see her face as she replied, 'Yes, I did know that, but Testament still felt like a place where I could make a home for myself and the baby. The town's big enough for there to be good schools, yet small enough for most people to know each other. As a single mother, I thought that was important—that the baby, as she grew, would know the names of the people in the street, and they'd know her and look out for her. I knew once the original tutting stopped, the locals would gradually come to accept me—and they'd know the baby from her birth, so she'd be a local. What I did miscalculate—'

She stopped and Grant wondered what had happened. Had to know.

'What?' he demanded.

She shrugged and a rueful glimmer of the radiant smile he'd seen earlier lit her eyes.

'Well, down in the city I was always hearing about the unemployment crisis in the country and I assumed, when I got here, it would be easy, finding a nanny for the baby. I didn't want a professionally trained person, just a nice grandmotherly type who'd had kids of her own and knew which end did what. I'd employ her during my working hours and have a couple of high school girls on standby for weekends and after hours, and all would be well.'

'Didn't happen, huh?'

Kate shook her head, the glimmer gone, leaving her eyes more sad than sober.

'One woman came in response to my ad, and she'd have minded the baby, but wouldn't do washing or even the lightest of housework. I didn't want her washing down the walls, just throwing a few nappies into the machine. I mean, with a baby this size who sleeps all the time, what was she going to do all day? *And* she wanted more money than trained nurses make at the hospital.'

'And no one else applied?'

Kate shook her head.

'Vi's got feelers out, but so far she hasn't come up with any solution. I just hope there's not some kind of embargo in place, because I turned down the first applicant.'

Grant shook his head, puzzled by the reaction as he, too, knew of the unemployment problems in regional areas. More than puzzled by the scrunching feeling around his heart as he'd listened to the doubt and hesitation in Kate's words.

It was probably pity. Pity for an old friend was acceptable—almost obligatory in fact. Though with an old friend like Katie, it was probably best she didn't see it—pity would be the last thing she'd accept. Visions of the meat cleaver rose obligingly in his head.

'So what are you going to do if Vi doesn't come up with someone?' he asked. There was more to this knight business than he'd originally thought.

'While she's little I can manage. Take her to the surgery or on calls when it's not too hot to have her in the car. Tara's available after school and at weekends and once school finishes next week, she'll come when I need her through the eight weeks of the Christmas holidays.'

'And then?'

Katie shrugged but the smile reappeared, sparkling in her eyes and seeming to shine in her skin.

'I'll have to get a city girl up here, and won't that stir the locals? As well as an unemployment problem here, there's a woman shortage. I'll have every young bachelor in town and out of it hanging around—like when a new clutch of female schoolteachers arrives. I could possibly set up as a marriage agency as a sideline—bringing young women to town on a regular basis, checking their household and baby-minding skills, then marrying them off with a good reference.'

'Not very good for Rose, all those changes in her life.'

'Rose?' Katie shrieked. 'I thought we'd ruled out flowers, days of the week, months of the year, seasons and anything that sounds like a mood or emotion.'

'You suggested Rose,' Grant retorted. 'Anyway, there are some nice names included in that sweeping embargo. And I thought you hated lists, and here you are, listing all the no-nos to me.'

'That wasn't a list—it was a statement. Lists presuppose an order—a first, second, third.'

Grant chuckled.

'I can't believe this! Was there ever a time we didn't argue?'

She shook her head, so the bright sunlight streaming into the kitchen made glints of gold dance through the curly tresses of hair. An almost overwhelming urge to run his fingers through it—to feel the warmth where the sun was touching—made him wonder, yet again, if the knight thing had been such a good idea.

He reminded himself of why he was here and began to ask questions about the hospital, eventually wondering what it had been like from a patient's point of view.

'Don't ask,' Katie muttered, when he asked the question aloud. 'Though to be fair, I didn't get much chance to test things out.'

She sighed, then, with the honesty he'd always admired in her, added, 'When Paul left, I intended going to Craigtown when the time came, then the baby was early, and to give Sister Clarke her due, she's a wonderful midwife, but I discharged myself as soon as possible. It was driving me nuts—all their "plural" stuff. We should do this and we should do that and how are we feeling today. I know I was still the size of two normal people, but there was only one of me, and a not very happy one at that.'

Grant found himself laughing, imagining Katie's ire at such behaviour.

'But admit it, Katie, you've probably done it yourself. We've all been guilty of it at some stage of our careers.'

'Not me!' she retorted. 'Not once—never!'

And Grant laughed again, but this time with the sheer pleasure of being with her again, with the old Katie who'd stood up for herself—and all her friends—and who'd been willing to take on the world, if necessary, to defend what she saw as right.

'I guess you told them what you thought of it as well,' he said, when his laughter had died down sufficiently for him to speak.

'Well, yes, I did. I wasn't feeling particularly well. You don't, you know, after a long labour during which the entire support staff have done the "we" thing. So when someone came in before dawn next morning and said it was time for us to have a nice sponge bath I told her what I thought of people who couldn't use a patient's name, and that individual patients were singular not plural, then I told her where to stick her sponge, picked up the baby and came home.'

'And you wonder why no one wants to work for you?'

He'd meant it as a joke, which he regretted as soon as he saw the stricken look on her face.

'I'm sorry,' he said, hoping to make amends, 'but you must admit, you probably didn't leave them with the impression you'd be a cheerful, happy, easy-to-get-on-with employer.'

'You're right,' she admitted, 'though I'd forgotten all about that little tantrum until now.' She gave a little laugh. 'When I think about it, I must have looked a right sight. Because the baby had come early I hadn't taken a bag to the hospital, so I was wearing a hospital-issue gown, one of those that comes together on one shoulder and down one side with Velcro, and it was flapping open, the baby was ready for a feed and screaming, and I couldn't find where they'd put my shoes so went barefoot, then foolishly left the path and stepped on every pebble in the backyard so I was hopping about like a madwoman.'

'Then, no doubt, you had to go back and face them all to reclaim your clothes.'

She nodded, cheeks becoming pink at the recollection.

'Had to go back to see a patient, in fact, though I did get dressed and put on sandals before I went. Sister Clarke did her "really, Dr Fenton" thing and told me the nurse I'd yelled at was so upset she'd had to go home, and that had mucked up the nursing schedule until two thousand and ten.'

'Sister Clarke obviously hasn't improved,' Grant said, with such empathy in his voice Kate felt something, probably left over from her youth or perhaps to do with the loneliness she'd been feeling, tug at her heart.

But whatever it was, she had to ignore it. Grant was an

old friend, and it would be good to have him—or anyone—here for a while, to help with the work while she adapted to life with the baby and the Health Department appointed a new hospital doctor. But he'd be going away again, so getting too dependent on his friendship would be a *bad thing*, and feeling heart-tugs for someone who had a Linda-Chlorinda stashed away back in the city was *an even worse* thing.

Thinking about Grant's fiancée made her stomach tighten, but she couldn't help but wonder...

No! Wondering about anything connected with Grant's personal life was definitely off-limits. Think of something else. Anything!

Baby names?

'I might make a list,' she said, startling Grant with his fork midway to his lips. 'Of baby names I quite like,' she explained. 'That way, if you persist in addressing her by name, I won't be constantly appalled.'

'Good move,' he said, but the lips, still awaiting the forkload of food, twisted upward at the corners and seemed to quiver as if holding back a smile might soon prove too much.

The teenage Grant Bell had had killer lips, but these full-grown features were even better. Full, but not too full, beautifully shaped and clearly delineated by a neat, pale rim, so in a lip contest he'd have to be a frontrunner. And they were ultra-mobile as well—ready to smile, or open in a shout of laughter.

'Yo, Katie? You still with me here? We were going to make a list.'

His words brought her abruptly out of her contemplation of lip structure, though not completely.

'Have you been in touch with Linda? What does she do? Is she a doctor? Does she live in Sydney?'

His startled look told her she'd asked far too many questions—showed way too much interest. While the sensible

Kate who resided in her head was scoffing at her lack of moral fibre, allowing killer lips to distract her.

'I thought we were discussing baby names,' he reminded her. 'I've a pencil and a paper. I'm ready.'

He managed to sound hurt, an act she didn't believe for a moment, but as he obviously wasn't going to answer her questions about the woman in his life, she might as well go with the baby-naming option.

'I quite like Sophie.'

'I've already got that down. Come on, there must be more than one—though if there isn't then Sophie she'll have to be.'

'No, it's not quite right. What other girls' names are there? You must have been out with dozens of women— what were their names? Apart from Linda, because I'd always think of the Chlorinda thing, and I must add I find it very strange, considering you used to tell me about all the girls at school with whom you were passionately in love— before you and me...you know—that you're being so close-lipped about her.'

The 'lip' word made her look at his again, and this time she shivered, remembering, just before those lips had touched hers the first time, him saying he'd only talked about the other girls to make her jealous.

She'd wanted to believe it then, but didn't need to now.

'I once took out a Rachel—do you want it on the list?'

'Rachel? Rache? Would that morph to Roach so the poor thing would be known as either a cockroach or an iffy cigarette?'

Grant crossed out 'Rachel'.

'Let's go alphabetically. Anna, Annabel, Alison, Archimedes?'

'You're being silly now,' Kate said crossly. 'I told you I didn't like lists—and this is why. I know I suggested it, but I'm no good at it.'

'Don't you have a book with baby names in it?'

She looked at him with wide-eyed surprise.

'And where would I get one of those? At the local newsagent so everyone in town would know I didn't have a name picked out for the baby?'

'They all know by now, anyway,' Grant said gently. 'Every patient I saw this morning asked if you'd decided yet.'

Katie shrugged as if the whole conversation was aggravating her, then got up and began to clear the table.

'Megan. I'll call her Megan. Or will that clash with Fenton? Megan Fenton? Isn't there a rule about having a different number of syllables in each part of the name, though you've got one and one and it suits you.'

Grant stood up and carried his plate to the sink. He set it down, put his hands on Katie's shoulders and turned her so he could look directly at her.

'Don't panic about this, Katie. There's no rush and there are no rules. She's your baby, and you can call her what you like and take as long as you like deciding, though she'll hate you if you're still calling her ''the baby'' or, even worse, just ''baby'' when she goes to school.'

He received a wobbly smile for his efforts.

'I tell you, Grant, this motherhood caper is for the birds. I seem to be managing my learnt skills like doctoring just fine, but as far as everyday living goes?' She shook her head. 'Whatever neurones I possessed have closed down, and my body seems to have reverted to automatic responses that come from primitive instinct, before *Homo sapiens* developed the skill to reason.'

'Sometimes it might be best not to reason,' he said softly, then, because she was so goldenly beautiful, so soft to the touch, and so very, very familiar, he leaned forward and kissed her on the lips.

Beneath his fingers, he felt her shoulders stiffen, then an almost imperceptible relaxation of the muscles as her lips moved against his, not exactly responding but definitely not drawing away.

Sanity returned in time for him to do the drawing away.

'You taste the same, Katie Fenton,' he said, hoping lightness might carry the day, while his head berated him for his folly and reminded him he had no excuse, like recent childbirth, to explain why he'd given way to primitive instinct.

'You say that as if people taste different,' she said grouchily. 'All skin's made up of the same chemical and molecular composition, so there shouldn't be a difference.'

'There is if someone's been eating a lot of garlic. Don't tell me you can't taste it in the sweat,' he argued out of habit, and because it saved him thinking about his body's reaction to kissing Katie.

'I haven't ever licked the sweat off a garlic-eater so I wouldn't know,' she said, with sufficient huffiness for him to wonder if she, too, had been disturbed by the kiss.

Physically disturbed?

'And shouldn't you be heading off to the butcher's? The baby will wake any minute, expecting to be fed, so I can't come with you, but remember, my cooking skills are restricted to throwing something under a grill, or into a frying-pan, or on a barbecue. Words like ''braising'' bring on heart palpitations.'

'I told you I'll do the fancy stuff,' Grant promised, realising it was a good idea to get away from her while he worked out why he'd given in to the urge to kiss her—and how he could prevent it happening again.

He was out the back door when she called him back.

'Wait. I didn't give you money. And we haven't talked about pay or board or the patients you saw or any of the things we should have talked about at lunchtime. You diverted me with baby names and now look where we are!'

He grinned at her.

'Calm down—we have all afternoon to talk. It's Monday

and, according to Vi, you don't have afternoon surgery on a Monday—just an evening session, six to eight.'

'Oh!' Kate said, because there didn't seem to be anything else to say. Then she remembered the money again but it was too late. He was already crossing the paddock at the back of the hospital, taking the short cut everyone used to reach the shops.

She pushed her hands through the thick mass of her hair, and for the thousandth time since summer had begun she considered getting it cut. But growing her hair long again had been the first of her post-Mark rebellions. He'd always insisted she keep it short— 'I mean to say, Kate, a mop like that just won't fit into a theatre cap, now, will it?'

No, she wouldn't cut her hair, but she'd have to do something about the brain-drain she was experiencing. Perhaps it was the heat, as well as the after-baby problem, that was causing her neurones so much trouble.

Though she doubted she could blame the weather for her reaction to Grant's kiss, for the sizzle it had caused deep in her abdomen, and the fiery rush of longing that had triggered a trembling in her limbs and a pit-a-pat of uncertainty in her heartbeats. Maybe the heat and longing she remembered from the long-ago relationship hadn't been anything to do with their age...

Maybe it was to do with some special chemical balance between the two of them...

But Grant's presence was temporary, *and* he was engaged to another woman, and even if he'd been available, there was the baby to consider...

With confusion raging in her head, Kate pressed her hand to her chest. Perhaps if she could regulate the still uneven thumping of her heart she'd be able to think more clearly.

It didn't help so, because her knees remained unreliable, she sat down.

That didn't help either.

Distraction—she needed distraction!

Maybe she *should* get into lists. She could start with one of things to do—discuss wages with Grant, discuss board with Grant, discuss division of labour with Grant, ditto patients, ditto kissing. No, no more kissing, and definitely no discussion of it.

Grant was here as a friend, doing a favour for his aunt. Temporarily here. And Grant had a Linda he didn't want to discuss, so even if Kate wanted a man, which she didn't, Grant wasn't the one, which was just as well as he'd already admitted he was in medicine for the money he could make, and she could never marry someone who saw the career she loved as nothing more than a means to an end.

Although if the end was buying back the family property, or replacing it with another one, surely that was allowable, if not admirable...

She frowned out into the garden. Was making money with a reason behind it better than making money for the sake of it? Mark was in medicine for the money, as were a lot of his friends. Money had been the reason Mark had wanted her to specialise. But Grant?

Recalling the 'making money to buy back the farm' conversation they'd had, she remembered it had shifted focus. She'd sensed Grant's initial aim was no longer relevant, or that his career now had another goal—something he hadn't wanted to discuss.

Something to do with the sadness she caught glimpses of behind the twinkle in his eyes?

Or maybe Linda didn't like cattle.

The baby's cry roused her from the pointless speculation, and by the time she'd changed and fed the wee darling and popped her, sleepily digesting her tucker, back to bed, the subject of her musings had returned and she went out to have the talk they should have had earlier.

Was it because she'd been studying his lips earlier that she found it so hard to concentrate? OK, so they'd settled on a reasonable recompense for him, and on who'd do which surgery sessions. She'd, reluctantly, agreed he could mind the baby while she worked a couple of sessions a week, though she'd insisted Vi would manage if he wanted to get out of the house, perhaps have a look around the place, explore old haunts.

She'd even managed to retain most of what he'd told her about the patients he'd seen that morning, but throughout it all a separate part of her mind had been cataloguing his features, checking out the strong, straight nose, with enough of a flare to the nostrils to make it distinctively attractive. And the eyebrows—thick but nicely shaped, arching neatly over those incredible blue eyes.

So far, she'd managed to avoid too close a study of the eyes, though she suspected she'd get there eventually.

And find them shuttered against her?

'Are you listening?'

'Y-yes, yes, of course I was,' she stammered, more flustered than she cared to admit. 'You were talking about Mrs Milward, your old Grade Two teacher. She was gone before I came to Testament, though I'd already done Grade Two by then.'

The lips she'd given an A-plus to earlier twisted into a funny kind of smile.

'Mrs Milward was three patients ago. I thought you'd zoned out on me. Go and have a sleep, Katie. I picked up a baby-name book at the newsagent, and I'll go through it and write down names you might like.'

She should have said, Don't bother, and reminded him the baby's name had nothing to do with him, and probably suggested he go out somewhere—look up old friends—but somehow the concept of Grant buying her a baby-name book, together with the A-plus lips, had sent what useful bits of brain she retained into a spin, and having a sleep seemed like an excellent idea.

Grant watched her go and sighed with a release of tension he hadn't been aware he'd been feeling. This rescue scenario wasn't playing out the way he'd expected. The kiss had been bad enough but, OK, that was a mistake he could live with, but after he'd made his escape, and cooled down on his walk across the back paddock—cooled down metaphorically, not physically as it was hotter than Hades out there—he'd been thrown back into chaos at the butcher's.

His murderous feelings towards Mick Gazecki, who'd winked at him and made lewd suggestions about how sexy new mothers usually felt, had made him realise Katie's impulse to brain the butcher with his own meat cleaver had some merit.

He'd even gone so far as to eye the implement in question.

The heat must be getting to him. He needed something to do.

He'd put away the meat earlier, dividing it into portions and freezing most of it, though he'd decided to use the mince tonight. He could do that now. Make a pasta sauce and shove it in the fridge until the evening surgery finished. He could reheat it while he cooked the pasta. He assumed she did have pasta.

He checked the pantry, and there among the basics found an open packet of little pasta bows that had possibly been there since Dr Darling's time.

Not that pasta suffered much with keeping. The corner store where he shopped when home probably had older stuff on its shelves.

But while his mind tried to stay focussed on the merits of aged pasta and the construction of a suitable sauce to accompany it at dinner-time, another part of it was recalling the softness of Katie's lips, the luminous quality of her skin, the way her eyes caught and held his, the brash confidence in them undermined by an apprehension he guessed only he could see.

He was standing in the pantry, pasta packet in hand, when she came, soft-footed, back into the kitchen.

'I'm just getting a drink of water,' she explained, but now there was more apprehension than confidence in those fascinating eyes, and he waited, knowing she'd eventually get to what she'd come to say.

'I drink a lot—it's something I vaguely remember from the early Obs and Gyn lectures, about nursing mothers needing to keep the fluids up. I don't think we should kiss any more.'

And with that she was gone, leaving him wondering if she'd really tacked that embargo on the end of a statement about the fluid intake of nursing mothers.

He made to follow her, then realised it would be a mistake. But standing in the pantry with a packet of pasta in his hand wasn't much use either. He returned the packet to the shelf, checked on the other ingredients he'd need, then walked through to the bedroom with the floral sheets.

He had plenty of time before he needed to start cooking. He'd get his leathers and take the bike out—tool around the country, visit old haunts as Katie had suggested. Ride past the old property and see how it looked.

Banish a few ghosts.

He pulled on his leather pants, then boots, and lastly shrugged into the jacket. It was too hot for full leathers, but experience told him only speed would do at times like this and he wasn't stupid enough to risk it without some protection.

But a new ghost rode right along with him. The friend of his childhood, the Katie he'd first known—laughing, joking, daring and being dared. The slim, vibrant Katie who'd suddenly, that long-ago Christmas holidays, grown breasts and hips and had made his loins ache just being near her. Who'd become more than a friend, firing his blood to madness with her kisses, entering passionately into their first explorations of their sexuality.

The real Katie, today's Katie, was different. For a start, she had a lush, full, womanly body, and it was, once again, having an unfortunate effect on his loins.

But she also had a baby, he reminded himself as he passed beyond the limits of the town and opened the throttle on the bike, hoping speed might banish his uncertainties and blow away the memories.

Though he knew he couldn't outrace all of them. Hadn't he tried it before? He eased back before the bike reached top speed and rode more cautiously, enjoying the rush of fresh-scented air, the sight of wide paddocks stretching out on either side of the road, white-faced cattle resting beneath shady trees, lifting their heads to watch him pass.

CHAPTER SEVEN

LIFE settled into a routine. Baby names were added and crossed off the list that wasn't really a list, and Katie began not only to feel human but to fret about not doing more.

Especially when Grant had free time, because being with him, whether in the house talking over the day, or out of it walking the baby or going for drives to places they'd frequented as children, was making her think things she shouldn't think. Being with him was giving her an idea of family that was dangerous in the extreme as Grant would be gone within weeks and she'd be more alone than ever.

'I've found a phone number for an agency in Brisbane,' she announced, when he came back from surgery to join her for lunch on the fourth Monday of his stay.

'Looking for another locum? What did I do wrong?'

His teasing smile caused heart problems which were another reason she should be doing more. It was having so little to do that had her mind thinking things it shouldn't think, while Grant's constant presence had her body behaving in ways that the new mother in her found shockingly irresponsible.

'I need a nanny, not another locum. Vi's come up with one or two possibilities, but one lass is engaged to a young man in Craigtown and will be moving away as soon as they're married, and the other is just the kind of woman I want but she's planning a three-month trip overseas early in the new year. And also, I don't know if a live-in mightn't be better—for call-outs.'

'Vi was talking about Mrs Carter, the woman who's going overseas. I don't know about her. One of my younger sisters was at school with a Carter and I'm sure Sue said Mrs Carter used to beat her kids.'

'Mary Carter? That can't possibly be right.'

'OK, not beat them but wave a wooden spoon at them,' Grant conceded, though why he felt obliged to throw a spanner in the 'nanny' works, he wasn't sure. Looked at sensibly, having someone else in the house, if only during the day, was a good idea. It would provide a kind of buffer zone between himself and Katie, so maybe his body would stop reacting to her presence and his mind stop thinking things it shouldn't think.

'All our mothers waved wooden spoons at us as kids—it was the ultimate threat. Mum's actually connected with the back of my legs from time to time, and I don't think it's done me any irreparable damage.' She paused, then half smiled as she added, rather sadly, 'Though maybe Mum thinks it has. Or maybe she's thinking she didn't do it often enough.'

'What's happened between you?'

Grant hadn't realised he was going to ask the question, but there'd been so much pain in Katie's words, he'd blurted it out.

She hesitated, sighed, then said softly, 'She's old-fashioned, I guess. And me coming back to Testament made things worse. You know what Mum was like. Underneath, she'd do anything for anyone, but she did tend to lord it over people. She always had a huge sense of her own importance. If I'd taken off for Craigtown, pregnant and unwed, she'd probably have reacted better, but coming here…'

'But she will come? They'll come? When they come home from their trip?'

Katie nodded.

'Of course. After all, it's likely to be their only grandchild, but, well… It's my fault, too,' she said, her voice thick with the emotion she was trying hard to hide. 'We argued, Mum and I—back in the beginning—and I said things I shouldn't have said, things about her marriage.'

She looked up at him, then admitted, 'You know me—act first and think later.'

Grant, who'd been about to question the 'only grandchild' statement, found he was more intrigued by the final admission and set the other remark aside for consideration later.

'What kind of things?'

He saw a smile flicker on her lips, although the sadness in her eyes remained.

'Stuff that must have been stewing for a long time, but was probably quite wrong—like wanting more than she and Dad had had from marriage. More than mutual affection and respect, which was all I had for Mark. In fact, as our relationship continued I didn't even have the respect part, and though I probably would have married him to give the baby a father, and made a go of it, the way Mum and Dad had, I'm sure I'd have always felt something was missing.'

This time her smile was warmer, and cheekier, and it did things to his intestines he didn't want to think about.

'All in all, it was probably a good thing he made having an abortion a condition of us getting married, then was so adamant about not having anything to do with the baby if I went ahead with the pregnancy. It got Mark out of my life, though it did cause problems between me and Mum.'

There was a silence as he ate the sandwich she'd prepared, while she cut hers into little pieces then rearranged them on the plate, as if by shifting them she'd fool him into thinking she was eating.

'You'll sort it out,' he said, speaking gently—wanting to make things right for her.

She nodded.

'I know. After all, as I keep telling myself, we're both adults.' Then, with typical Katie-bravado she added, 'Though getting Mum to agree with that isn't easy.'

She ate a minute piece of sandwich then looked up at Grant.

'Do you think I'll be the same? Is mothering a hereditary trait? Will I be able to accept the baby's old enough to make her own decisions when she's, what? Fourteen? Eighteen? Twenty-six?'

'Never, if you're still calling her "the baby",' Grant told her. 'And I think decision-making is something that you learn as you grow and develop. Take a six-month-old tasting solids for the first time—if he decides he doesn't like them, splat, they're spat right back at you. Two-year-olds can probably decide whether they want jam or peanut butter on their toast, four-year-olds know if they play with the hose and get all their clothes wet, they'll be in trouble, so have to decide if the fun is worth it.'

Kate heard the words, but underlying them was something she didn't understand. Though one thing was certain—Grant wasn't winging this conversation. He'd thought it through, considered it, worried about decisions and responsibilities himself.

'Does Linda have a child?'

She didn't know why she'd asked, but as soon as the words were spoken, she knew they'd have been better left unsaid. Grant's expression changed from a momentary perplexity to understanding to pain. He shook his head, added 'No' in case she didn't understand head shakes, then he pushed back his chair, stood up, muttered something about a note he'd forgotten to write at the surgery and walked out.

You're here to help Katie, not add to her burdens by dumping your baggage on her, he told himself fiercely, striding across to the surgery and unlocking the door. What he had to do was find someone to take care of the baby, so Katie could ease back into work; then, once she was happy with the arrangement, he could get out of town.

If the young woman who was getting married later next

year could work until Mrs Carter came back from overseas…

Or would a trained nanny from the city be better? Someone who'd been to nanny school and knew all the right things to do?

He thought back to couples he knew who'd employed these paragons, and remembered a discussion he'd had with one of the employers. Phoned the house.

'A city nanny would have to live in,' he said to Kate, then smiled to himself as he imagined her mental adjustment. 'And from what I've heard, they need their own space, a kind of bed-sitting room and *en suite*. Definitely their own bathroom. Have you thought of that?'

'They need an *en suite*?' she repeated, in tones of such disbelief he had to smile. 'But I haven't got an *en suite*!'

The expletive she wasn't going to use again was quickly followed by, 'Jeez Louise! I hadn't even thought of bathrooms. I mean, a live-in is good from the point of view of having someone here if I'm called out, but if they have to have a bathroom…'

There was a pause, then she asked, 'Why are we talking on the phone? Have you a lot of paperwork to do? I said I'd do all of that. I'm bored rigid doing nothing, and the house is so clean it's starting to feel like one of those display places.'

Another pause.

'Only they usually have two bathrooms, don't they?'

And on that note she hung up.

Grant knew he should stay away, even take off on the bike, but he was drawn back to the house by the same irresistible attraction that led moths to a light.

Kate was in the third bedroom. She had pinned her hair up so it was doing its 'falling down all over' thing again, and in the loose curls behind her ear he could see the end of a pencil. In one hand she held a tape measure and in the other a piece of paper.

'You'd think they'd make measuring tapes longer than a metre,' she complained, as she scratched a mark on the carpet then moved the tape along.

'They do,' Grant told her. 'You buy them at hardware shops, though the idea that you'd own such a thing as a tape measure intrigues me no end. One usually associates such things with button bottles and sewing baskets, and I remember you loathed sewing as much as you hated cooking when you were younger and had to do it at school.'

'But I did have a sewing basket,' she told him primly, moving the tape again then searching for her pencil to write something down. 'Still have it, though I doubt I've used it from that day to this. Can you see my pencil?'

'It's in your hair, but there's an easier way to do this, unless you want the measurements exact to the last centimetre.'

She straightened so she was squatting on her heels, pulling the short shorts very tight across firm buttocks.

'I'll step it out,' Grant said, desperate to distract his mind from that part of Katie's anatomy—any part of Katie's anatomy. 'I assume we're doing this to see if we can fit another bathroom in here. There, it's three metres by about three and a half, not big enough for a decent bedroom and an *en suite*. And though a second bathroom is an excellent idea, are you sure you want someone living in?'

She reached out a hand and he pulled her up, though that was a mistake as any time she was within arm's length he had a terrible urge to kiss her.

An urge not much diminished by the frown she was directing his way.

'Why shouldn't I?' she said. 'Have you heard horror stories of people with live-in help? Are there implications I should know about?'

Grant hesitated, mainly because the remark had been instinctive. *He* wouldn't want anyone living in—not in a house this size where someone else would be...

Would be what? he asked himself. A barrier between you and Katie? A curb on your lustful thoughts?

Get real here, mate. A live-in help is just what Katie needs.

And you won't be here, remember?

But no amount of talking convinced him, deep down in his gut, that it was the right move.

'Well, while I'm here the nanny thing isn't a problem, so you don't have to decide immediately. But a spare bathroom's good. Let's walk right through the house and see if we can't figure out the best place for it.'

'I thought I already had,' Kate muttered to herself, but she went along with him, mainly because she was puzzled by his failure to answer her live-in nanny questions, and was more concerned with figuring out why than with asserting her authority over where the bathroom should go in *her* house.

Apart from the fact a city girl might hate the country and the baby might have to put up with a few of them before one eventually stuck, having live-in help seemed a great idea.

The baby!

She really should choose a name—now she wasn't so sleep-deprived and her body had settled into the routine of feeding.

'What was the name you suggested yesterday?'

They were in Grant's bedroom now, and Kate realised she hadn't been in here since he'd arrived. She looked around, seeing how tidy he kept it, smelling the air, which was definitely different—decidedly male.

'We're talking about bathrooms, not names at the moment,' he reminded her. 'And as this is the largest of the bedrooms, it would probably be most suitable to convert into a kind of bed-sitting room. See, you could take part of that wall out and put a small *en suite* in there, plus a dressing room. You'd lose that small bedroom, but you'd still have three. One for you, one for the baby—Caroline was yesterday's name—and one for the nanny or for visitors.'

'So I couldn't have both at once,' Kate said, though she was thinking more of how strange it felt to be in a male's bedroom—in Grant's bedroom, as it was right now. 'The nanny and visitors.'

But her eyes were drawn to Grant's bed, and she was imagining him lying there.

Naked...

'Shortened to Carrie, or Cassie, or even Caz, and all of them are OK.'

She blinked away an image of a naked Grant and peered suspiciously at him.

'Weren't we talking about bathrooms?'

His grin suggested they'd moved on from that conversation some time ago.

'Yes, we were, but you'd lost that particular plot so I assumed you were thinking of the other conversation we were kind of conducting. Baby names? Caroline? Not bad when shortened?'

'Is it wrong for me to want to go to bed with you?'

The question came so completely out of the blue, Grant could only stare at her.

'Well, not especially with you, but with anyone. Shouldn't my sexuality be in abeyance when I've just given birth and am feeding a very young infant? Do you know anything at all about it? Perhaps I should look it up? Would I find it in a medical book, or would it be under psychology?'

And whether to suit action to the words, or to go off on some equally bizarre quest, Grant couldn't tell, but she left the room without waiting for an answer to any of her questions, which was just as well, for it could be a day or two before he recovered sufficiently to even gabble out a reply.

'The problem is,' Kate told the baby as she bathed the little body, 'I was so used, when I was growing up, to talking about anything and everything with Grant. Arriving in town in the summer holidays, and Dad having meetings with his father, he was about the first kid I met. From that time, he kind of took care of me, making out I was a nuisance but looking out for me anyway. Especially when I started high school, and was too big for my boots and always getting into trouble.'

The baby kicked at the water as if to agree with what had been said, but didn't offer much else in the way of an opinion.

'And the other problem is,' she added, while silently marvelling at the perfection of miniature toes and toenails, 'that when I considered our future, yours and mine, building a life together here in the country, I never considered for an instant that I might ever feel sexy again. I mean I hadn't—with Mark—not for a long time, and I thought it was probably age or that women didn't feel an urge for sex the way men did, especially as they got older. So this attraction thing is just so totally unexpected—and definitely unacceptable, given all the circumstances.'

The baby offered no opinion on female sexuality so Kate sighed and resolutely turned her thoughts to more practical stuff.

'Would you like to be called Caroline? While you're small, and the name's a bit grand, we could call you Cassie. Would you like that?'

A smile she knew wasn't really a smile hesitated on the tiny pink lips and, in the surge of excitement the almost-smile generated, Kate called for Grant to come.

'Look, she almost smiled. I called her Cassie—well, I suggested it to her—and she really did smile.'

'Is that why you yelled? I thought something terrible had happened.'

'I didn't yell, I called,' Kate argued. 'And I thought you might be interested.'

Though now he was here, splashing water on the baby—

yes, Caroline shortened to Cassie might work well—Kate remembered her previous conversation with the man, and regretted the yell—call.

'Aren't all smiles put down to wind until the baby's, what—six weeks old, is it?'

'How could she have wind when she hasn't been fed? And anyway, five weeks isn't so far off six weeks,' Kate muttered, though why she felt compelled to argue with him was a mystery.

However, Grant seemed unperturbed, by both the argument and, apparently, her previous idiotic questions. He was catching the tiny feet as they splashed, and getting very wet in the process, and if the baby—Cassie—wasn't smiling, then she had a whole lot of wind.

'She might be precocious. What do I have to do with a precocious child? Do you accelerate them? Put them into programmes so they get maximum stimulation?'

These new worries brought on the familiar sense of panic over the future which Kate experienced so regularly she sometimes wondered if she could survive motherhood, but Grant was laughing—at her this time, not the baby.

'I don't think they're issues you need to address right now. I could be wrong, but I doubt they have stimulation programmes for bright five-week-olds.'

'You're right,' Kate admitted, feeling some relief but a new concern over the effect of Grant's laughter—here in her bedroom. 'And bath-time's over.'

She grabbed a towel she'd set out on the bed and bent to lift the baby from the small tub, but something went wrong, and though the baby ended up in the right place, in her arms, the tub upended itself, splashing across the bed.

'You are so totally disorganised,' Grant told her, grabbing other towels to mop up the mess. 'Why you set a bath on something as unstable as a bed is beyond me! As you haven't bothered to get proper nursery furniture, why don't you bath her on the kitchen table?'

Kate clasped Cassie—yes, it suited her—to her chest and glared at her accuser.

'I did until you came, then I thought you might think it wasn't too hygienic so I changed to doing it on the bed, and I haven't got proper nursery furniture because it's not the sort of thing you can buy in Testament, and what with taking over a very neglected practice and working out how to do the paperwork associated with being a single-practice GP, and Paul Newberry leaving, I didn't have time to go to Craigtown. Vi gave me the crib and after that...'

She'd started out mad, telling him off, but her confidence had oozed away so by the time she finished the little speech she sounded so uncertain that Grant wanted to put his arms around her and promise her he'd take care of everything.

But he couldn't do that. He was only a temporary solution, and if they got too close, his departure would leave her life even more barren than it had been before he'd arrived.

And if they got too close, his departure would undoubtedly leave *his* life more barren than it had been.

Though until his return to Testament, he'd doubted whether that would be possible.

'I'll chuck the towels into the washing machine—your sheets, too. They're soaked.'

He spoke because he had to say something to explain a hurried departure from the room, but in his heart he knew it was already too late—the getting-too-close thing. Knew his life was going to be more barren than it had been, when he left Testament and Katie.

For a brief moment, as he measured laundry liquid into the machine, he contemplated not leaving. Fear, terror, helplessness and grief—emotions he'd thought he'd conquered long ago—rose up to engulf him. Katie worried about how she might cope with an exceptional child, and whether she'd be too dominating a mother.

She didn't know the half of things there were to worry

about—things that clutched at your heart and drove you to the edge of madness with the pain they caused.

He started the machine, then, by way of insurance, walked back to the bedroom and poked his head through the door.

She was sitting on the driest part of the bed, her back propped on pillows, shirt unbuttoned, and Cassie was sucking greedily on one finely blue-veined breast. The image was so serenely beautiful it stole his breath, and it took a moment before he could speak.

'Sorry!' he said, more abruptly than he'd intended. 'I know you don't like being interrupted but I wanted to tell you I'm just popping over to the surgery. I meant to phone Linda this morning, then didn't get a chance. I'd use my mobile but the battery's flat and it's on the charger. I'll pay for the call, of course.'

He walked away, hoping he'd sounded sufficiently impersonal to undo any closeness that might have been developing between them. The Linda thing had been a masterstroke—if only he didn't keep forgetting to use it. He had to bring her up more often. And though he'd invented her originally to reassure Katie he was harmless—as far as being a man was concerned, Linda could now act as a suit of armour for himself.

Kate watched the door close behind him, and told herself she should be pleased he had a Linda. She also reminded herself it had been her own choice to go the single-mother route.

But enough of her brain was working for her to not believe a word of it. Far from not wanting him with her while she fed the baby, she'd positively ached to ask him to come in, to sit with her and chat, while Cassie—yes, that was the name—had her afternoon tea.

This was dangerous ground, and having Grant here for another however many weeks—she kept forgetting to ask

Vi what arrangements she'd made with him—was asking for trouble.

She lifted the sleeping baby to her shoulder, patted her half-heartedly in the hope she might burp, reminded herself of something she'd once read that said burping was useless anyway and put the little one—Cassie—down.

On the way through to the kitchen she grabbed a phone book and the notepad and pen she kept by the phone. She put on the kettle for a cup of tea, set the notepad on the kitchen table with the pen beside it and made a new resolution, though it was still three weeks to New Year.

'I will become organised and if that means becoming a list-maker, then so be it.'

Said out loud, the resolution sounded pathetic, but as no one was around to hear it didn't matter. Once her tea was made, she settled at the table and opened the phone directory at the Yellow Pages.

Would there be a listing for bathrooms, or would she have to get separate people in—a carpenter and a plumber, and possibly an electrician because the nanny would probably want a power-point for her hair-dryer? She wrote these trades down on her list, one beneath the other, and marvelled at how neat it looked and how proud of herself she felt.

And she'd need a painter—added painter to the list—although perhaps she could do that part herself. Keep her busy and out of Grant's way when he was home.

Crossed the painter off.

She checked the index, found bathrooms and turned to the right page, but most of the so-called 'bathroom renovations our specialty' ads had addresses in the city, and bringing them all this way would be expensive.

Perhaps if she phoned the nanny agency and checked on the bathroom thing first.

Wrote 'Phone agency' on the list.

She'd sound like a twit but it might save some money.

Money! She'd spent her savings and practically mortgaged her soul to get the house and practice.

Phone bank manager.

Somehow the thought of asking Brian for a loan made her feel queasy. It wouldn't feel right—having to admit to a patient you had so little in the way of financial stability you had to borrow for a bathroom.

She drew a line through the last item, then leafed through the book in search of finance companies.

Unfortunately for that idea, she could remember her bank manager father explaining how families like the Bells, who'd been on the land for generations, had been consumed by financial difficulties because they'd overextended themselves and borrowed through finance companies to stay afloat.

'It only prolongs the inevitable,' her father had said, as he'd tried to stem her rage and despair by explaining the bank's decision was unavoidable—and not his sole responsibility!

She wrote 'Phone Brian' on the list, because banks knew how far you could extend yourself without getting into serious trouble.

'Don't tell me you're writing a list!'

Grant's voice made her turn towards the back door, where he was standing regarding her, a teasing smile playing around the lips which had become the focus of her nightly dreams.

'I'm getting my life in order,' she told him. 'Kettle's boiled if you want a cup of tea. And Cassie's just gone off to sleep so she should be all right for an hour. If you've got nothing you want to do, could I leave her with you while I pop over to see Vi?'

His blue eyes narrowed with what looked like suspicion.

'I want to ask her who might be able to do the bathroom,' she added, though she didn't really need to explain to Grant why she was going.

'Fair enough,' he said, then he grinned at her. 'Just tell me. Is Cassie it, or are we just trying it on for a week?'

She had to smile—impossible not to.

'I think it's it,' she told him, while telling herself that, of course, it was possible to not smile back. 'But I guess we'll have to wait and see.'

She fled past him, out the door, because every minute she was near him she was at the mercy of her unreliable hormones—the ones with a direct line to her even more unreliable mouth which was likely to come out with something outrageous like, Let's go to bed—should she remain in his vicinity.

Grant watched her departure, telling himself this was good, then he saw the list and realised, if she was getting serious about a spare bathroom, she must be equally serious about a live-in nanny.

The thought depressed him for reasons he didn't want to consider, and the last name on the list— 'Brian' —underneath 'Bank Manager', which she'd crossed out, obviously feeling it was too impersonal—well, that just made him angry.

Was she going there now? Was the Vi story just a ruse?

He peered out the window, but couldn't see her, though if she'd gone uptown, rather than to Vi's, she'd have walked across the back paddock.

Wouldn't she?

He threw the cup of tea he'd made down the sink and went into the living room to brood.

CHAPTER EIGHT

BROODING produced no answers—mainly because Grant wasn't sure of the questions. Not all of them.

Maybe he'd cook instead.

But that didn't help because, after only three weeks in the house, he felt at home in Katie's kitchen, and feeling at home there was a dangerous concept—something he didn't want to consider, let alone brood over.

He was stirring his simmering stock when she returned, accompanied by an elderly man who greeted him with great affection.

'You don't remember me, do you?' the stranger said, 'but you were the best little builder's labourer I've ever had. Back when you were about four—before you went to school—and I put in the new shearers' quarters for your dad.'

'Mr McConagle? I *do* remember. Well, I remember a very kind and patient man who let me think I was helping. I had a great time and for years after was certain I was going to be a builder.'

'More a handyman than a builder,' Mr McConagle said. 'That's what people need out here. Someone who can turn his hand to anything. I suppose doctors in the country are a bit the same.'

'Or should be,' Katie said darkly.

'Well, let's have a look at the job,' Mr McConagle suggested, and Katie, after a quick 'Is it OK if we go into your room?' to Grant, led the handyman through the house.

Grant fell in behind then realised it was nothing to do with him so went back to stirring his stock, which didn't need stirring. The task also lacked any degree of job satisfaction as he kept wanting to know what was happening and wondering why he was getting uptight about a live-in nanny for Cassie.

'Mr McConagle says he can do it before Christmas,' Katie announced, beaming with pleasure as she returned, alone, to the kitchen to impart her news.

Then some of the delight faded, and her eyes took on the concern which seemed to be an almost permanent fixture.

'Though it will mean you moving into the smaller bedroom next to mine, and there'll be sawdust and stuff around. Do you mind? Do you think the sawdust will harm the baby? Oh, dear! How can one small baby cause disruption that's way out of proportion for its size?'

You don't know the half of it, and I pray you never do, Grant thought, but as he couldn't say it, he concentrated on practical matters.

'It shouldn't harm her, if you keep the bedroom door shut. You can take her over to the surgery or out somewhere else while Mr McConagle is doing noisy things.'

He pretended the stock required his attention, though it needed only to be left simmering and later strained.

'You didn't answer about moving into the smaller bedroom.'

'Only because I was thinking it might be easier if I move to Vi's. After all, you're going to be wanting the small bedroom for the baby soon, and while Mr McConagle's working here, you could start decorating it.'

'Decorating it?'

'The baby's room—ready for the baby to move into.' She looked so stunned by this concept he found himself adding, 'I'll give you a hand if you like.'

But he doubted Katie had heard. She was still staring at him—well, in his direction—but a blankness in her eyes suggested she wasn't seeing him.

'Why hadn't I thought of that? I haven't even bought a

mobile. She's got fluffy toys patients brought as gifts, but she'll need colour, stimulation.'

Now the eyes which still had the power to mesmerise him regained focus—him—and she stepped towards him.

'Grant, what's wrong with me? Why am I making such a hash of all this mother-thing? Am I just not cut out for it? Will I always be this way? Will Cassie suffer because of it?'

She was literally shaking with the fears her imagination was feeding her, and instinct made it impossible for Grant not to step forward and take her in his arms.

'Will you stop upsetting yourself with such nonsense?' he said, drawing her soft, still trembly body close against his, hoping to warm as well as reassure her. 'You'd have got to decorating the baby's room in time—just as you'll sort out the nanny thing eventually. There's no hurry—not while I'm here. Right now, your main concern is getting to know young Cassie and allowing her time to get to know you. And staying calm. That's another big job you have to do, so she feels secure and gets plenty of tucker.'

The trembling had stopped, and her warmth fed into his until he found it hard to tell where her body stopped and his began—except that his was the one now feeling more than comfort and responding to hers in ways that went far beyond friendship.

But he couldn't draw away too abruptly and hurt her feelings, so he kind of edged away, far enough to take her chin in his hand and tilt her head up towards him.

'Feeling better?'

A slight nod answered his question, but the doubtful expression lingering in her green eyes suggested she was still worrying.

'So smile for me,' he ordered, knowing he had to move farther away—and soon.

The smile was his undoing. It trembled, as her body had earlier, and failed to remove the apprehension in her eyes, so it occurred to him he might have to kiss the worries away.

As in 'kiss it better'.

This final excuse flitted through his mind as his lips closed on hers, then his mind fogged over and his body, held in check for so long, took over.

Kate felt his fingers slide into her hair as his hands framed her face. She felt gentleness in the lips touching hers, and understood it was a gesture—kindness—but her body, so long given over to carrying, then bearing and feeding the baby, wanted more, so she forgot about all the consequences—forgot where kissing Grant had led before—and kissed him back.

A big mistake, as the kissing reminded her body of other things it had been missing, and it pressed closer to his, demanding some of the attention her lips were currently giving and receiving. As if in answer to her silent demands, Grant's hands caressed her back, tucked her buttocks closer to his body, then he slid a hand between their bodies and gently grazed his fingers across her breast.

Someone, she suspected it might have been her, moaned with a mix of need and sensual delight, and as Grant tipped her back across the kitchen table and began to unbutton her shirt, she wanted him so badly she began to shake again.

Then, as suddenly as the kiss had started, it stopped, Grant pulling them both upright, setting her gently away from him, steadying her with his hands on her shoulders.

'Noises off!' he said by way of explanation, then he added grimly, 'Which is just as well!'

As he stepped towards the stove to rescue a pot that had boiled over and sent stock spluttering onto the hot-plate, Kate became aware of both the phone ringing and the baby crying.

Guilt slammed into her, and she ignored the phone, knowing Grant would answer it, and hurried to the bedroom. She was changing Cassie when he poked his head around the bedroom door.

'Tractor accident out at Nevertire, the driver's pinned by the legs. I'm on my way. You're OK to do the evening surgery?'

She nodded, but he hesitated, and Kate wondered if he was going to mention the kiss, but in the end he shook his head then said, 'Katie, it's no wonder you didn't have time to get ready for the baby. This practice might have the occasional lull but, if the last few weeks are any indication, I'm surprised you've managed as well as you have since the hospital doctor took off.'

Thinking about the necessity for a second doctor in town was infinitely preferable to thinking about the kiss, but it wasn't a problem she could solve.

And the kiss, or her reaction to it, kept intruding so it was only with an enormous effort of will she stopped herself dreaming of things that couldn't be.

She'd contact the Health Department again—hospital appointments usually began in January so surely they'd have someone lined up by now.

Inevitably, she thought of Grant, but he had Linda stashed away in Sydney and some job awaiting him there. Quite what job, Kate hadn't yet managed to fathom, though from time to time she'd led the conversation close enough for him to say.

Which was strange, now she considered it. Grant had always talked about his plans and dreams. Growing grass that could withstand drought, turning around the rivers which wasted their water by flowing into the sea so they flowed inland to the thirsty land. They were ideas Australians had played with for generations, but still seductive enough for an enthusiastic teenager, always brimful of plans for the future.

Now, although she sensed a purpose in him—knew there was a deadline to his stay in Testament so there had to be a job of some kind waiting for him—he certainly wasn't talking about it.

Because it meant a lot to him?

She nodded to herself. Yes, that fitted. It was probably also why he rarely mentioned Linda.

She meant too much to him.

The idea was so depressing she sighed as she rocked Cassie's crib, though she had no right to be getting maudlin over Grant Bell's future career or personal relationships.

It was the kiss that had done it—made her think things she shouldn't think about the man who was helping her out of a very difficult situation. A man who'd given up his holidays to come to her rescue. And what did she know of relationships anyway? She'd made a mess of the only serious one she'd had, and hadn't she come out here determined to make a secure and happy life for herself and Cassie? Wasn't that her goal? Hadn't she committed herself to be the best single mother she possibly could be?

So why was she lusting over the first man who'd crossed her path? A man already engaged to someone else?

How responsible was that behaviour for a committed single mother?

She continued to scold herself even after Cassie dropped off to sleep, but as she wandered back to the kitchen she wondered if even committed single mothers might not be allowed a little daydream now and then…

Not if they involve Grant Bell, she answered herself firmly as she fixed a snack to eat before evening surgery.

When Grant still hadn't returned by the time she finished work, she had jam on toast for dinner, then went to bed, knowing he could be late and one of them should be getting some sleep.

But the question of what Grant planned to do after he left Testament lingered in her mind, so at breakfast next morning, when he'd filled her in on Kevin Cockburn's accident—crush fractures to both legs—and despatch to

Craigtown where he was then airlifted to Brisbane, she asked, 'I know you worked in A and E for three years. Was that leading somewhere? Are you going to specialise? Become an intensivist perhaps? Aren't they the newest "big thing"?'

He grinned at her but his eyes were shuttered, hiding whatever expression they might hold.

'They are, but it's not my career of choice.'

He continued eating his cereal as if he'd answered all her questions—not just the final one.

'Well?' she demanded.

This time he let her see his eyes, but there was something in the blueness she couldn't understand, though it did send a shivery sliver of ice along her veins.

'I'm going to specialise, yes. I start in the middle of January and, as I hadn't had a break for a few years, took a holiday rather than take a short contract somewhere. Which explains why I was at the beach and available for the summons from Aunt Vi.'

Which told Kate a lot she had known, some she hadn't and had avoided the main question quite neatly.

But she wasn't going to be put off.

'In what?' she demanded, pique at his evasion adding to her curiosity.

He sent her a puzzled look, so blatantly false she gritted her teeth so she wouldn't yell. 'What specialty?'

'Oncology. Paediatric oncology.'

He stood up as he said the first word, and crossed to the sink and was rinsing his cereal bowl as he added the further explanation.

Kate stared at him, aware of a shift in the balance between them, of a change in the atmosphere, more noticeable than a sudden drop in air temperature. Then Grant wiped his hands and walked out the back door, but whether he was heading for the hospital or the surgery, or even uptown, she had no idea.

The only thing she did know was that Grant was hurting.

She'd seen that same stiffness in his shoulders, the blankness in his eyes, way back when he'd had to leave his beloved home. And he'd coped by refusing to talk about it. By going to some place deep inside him, where even she hadn't been able to reach or follow. The memories were as clear as the leaves on the eucalypt outside the kitchen window.

But then she'd known what had happened—known the extent of his loss. Now all she had to go on was whatever they'd been discussing when the change had occurred.

Specialties.

Oncology.

Paediatric oncology?

She remembered the way he handled Cassie—with care, experience, even love, if she needed burping or changing. But putting her down as soon as the task was complete—not cuddling her or talking to her for too long. Staying aloof—apart.

Kate had assumed that while he was aware of a baby's needs, he just wasn't too fond of very small humans, and from time to time she had felt a little peeved he didn't show more wonder at the perfection of her daughter.

But if he was deliberately distancing himself...

For protection from some memories...

'D— Jeez Louise! Surely not!'

'Talking to yourself? Bad sign, Katie! I just popped over to the surgery to phone Brisbane. They're operating on Kevin's legs later this morning.'

Grant's sudden reappearance in the kitchen might have startled her, but not enough to miss the message he was giving her. He was over whatever had upset him and the subject was closed. Possibly for ever.

He put the kettle on to boil and popped a couple of slices of bread into the toaster. Watching him moving about her kitchen with such ease, undertaking simple domestic tasks, made her feel happy and empty at the same time.

Which was ridiculous!

'I hope it goes well,' she said, to show him she'd got the message, both messages—the one about the patient and the silent one—though she wasn't as certain she'd take much notice of the latter.

However, Kate was aware that now wasn't the time to push further, though there *was* something she wanted to talk to Grant about.

'Mr McConagle. We never finished that conversation—worked out about the new bathroom and where you'd sleep.'

Then she remembered why they hadn't finished the conversation, and heat crept into her cheeks.

'Gosh, is that the time? We'll have to talk about it later as one of us should be heading for work. I was going to go over and do some paperwork, but maybe I'd better spend the time sorting out the nanny *en suite* thing.'

But Grant didn't take the hint. He remained where he was, leaning against the sink, sipping tea and eating his toast while watching her with a frowning kind of academic interest, as if trying to remember who she was.

Grant knew he had to move, but it was difficult. Though staring at Katie wasn't producing answers so he may as well be working.

He finished his breakfast and walked across to the surgery, his mind still puzzling over why the question of a live-in nanny was bothering him.

Because once Katie had this paragon in place, she'd no longer need him?

No, it couldn't be that. He was going anyway.

He had to go.

Cassie was one baby, but the work he'd chosen to do might eventually save the lives of hundreds of babies.

Though the position on the team had been hotly contested and one of any number of able men or women could be chosen to take his place.

No!

The word sounded so loudly in his head he glanced around in case he'd actually said it aloud. But the birds in the cassia seemed unfazed, and the young mother dragging her toddler up the path towards the surgery's front door hadn't even glanced his way.

Loving a baby was like having your heart held to ransom. No way could he go through that again.

The mother with the toddler was his first patient—she was also pregnant according to the test kit she'd bought at the chemist.

'I didn't want another baby quite so soon,' she told Grant, though the pleasure in her eyes belied her words. 'But seeing as it's coming, is there any way I can have it here? Now you're here, surely it would be OK.'

Grant must have looked as puzzled as he felt for, without waiting for a response from him, she went right on talking. 'Dr Newberry, before Kate came, said it wasn't possible to have little Brendan here because, as the only doctor, he mightn't be around when I went into labour, but Mum says Dr Darling delivered all the babies in Testament for years, and he wouldn't always have been around when the mothers went into labour. I mean, given how long labour takes, it shouldn't have been a risk, but now there are two doctors—'

'I'm only temporary.' Grant blurted out the words, determined to stop this misconception before it went any further—or he felt any guiltier. 'But once a new hospital doctor is appointed it should be OK. I know Katie—Dr Fenton—is interested in the local women having their babies here. She's done a short obstetrics course and is really very keen. If you ask Vi, she can make sure you see Katie on your next appointment.'

The young woman smiled so broadly Grant wondered if

he'd overstated the case. And was Katie's desire to do obstetric work dependent on the appointment of a hospital doctor or would she go ahead anyway?

He completed his examination of the woman, made notes on her card, then saw her out.

Vi came in with some drug-test results.

'So Katie's organising a live-in nanny,' she said, and looked at Grant, obviously expecting some reaction.

'It's the sensible thing,' he said, quelling his own reservations about the move.

'I guess,' Vi said, though her tone was glum. 'But such a pity when she's obviously enjoying parenting, and I think, deep down, she'll hate handing so much of it over to someone else.'

'It was her decision to go along the path of single motherhood,' Grant reminded his aunt, though the gruffness in his tone was more to do with the bad feeling in his guts than with Katie's difficult choice.

He picked up the papers from the pathology lab and pretended to study them so Vi would realise the subject was closed.

Not that Vi would take any notice of something as subtle as a hint.

'Maybe marrying Brian wouldn't be such a bad idea. She'd have security so she wouldn't have to work full time for financial reasons, and she could get someone to take over the practice, just do a few surgeries a week and start up some of the ancillary things she feels are missing in the town.'

Vi walked away. Though Grant had heard the rest of the conversation, it hadn't made a lot of sense as the words 'marrying Brian' had kept hammering away in his head.

They were still echoing there, in spite of the demands and conversation of nineteen more morning patients, when he returned to the house for lunch. Katie was there, dressed not in her usual uniform of short shorts and a cropped top but in a flirty skirt with blue and yellow flowers on it and a yellow T-shirt which gave her skin a special golden glow.

There was a similar glow in her eyes…

She must have been out, and though he wanted to ask where—and perhaps why—the noise in his head took precedence.

'I thought you'd got rid of Brian,' he said, and saw the glow fade from her eyes and puzzlement take its place.

'Got rid of? Brian? What are you talking about?'

'Brian who was doing your lawns. I told you I'd do them. I did them last Saturday.'

'Yes?'

She sounded confused but it could be a ploy.

'So what's Vi talking about?'

Katie shook her head, making her curls dance and jiggle in a way that told him she'd washed her hair as well.

'Vi?' she asked, still sounding confused. 'What did Vi say?'

'That you were going to marry Brian?'

'Marry Brian? Brian Ridley? Vi said that?'

Her disbelief penetrated the cloud of anger and, yes, he had to admit to some confusion.

'Well, she mightn't have said exactly that, but she gave that impression.'

Katie stared at him as if unable to make sense of what he was saying, then she shook her head so the curls bobbed about again and distracted him.

'Nonsense!' she said. 'You've got it wrong. Maybe you're working too hard. I should have taken morning surgery. You had a late and stressful night last night with Kevin, and—'

'I am not overtired or overstressed!' Grant told her, speaking slowly and just a trifle loudly to make sure she understood. 'I simply don't think you should consider marrying a man like that. You've Cassie to think of, and she'll need someone with strength and character as a father, not some chinless wimp of a bank manager.'

It was the way she straightened up that told Grant he'd gone too far. Straightened up and looked at him, green eyes narrowed in anger.

'Before you get that foot out of your mouth and insert the other one, might I remind you that my father was a bank manager. And furthermore, Brian Ridley happens to have a most attractive chin, which, I might add, doesn't jut out stubbornly when he's arguing. He also has a nose that doesn't keep poking itself into other people's business. And if you're not overtired, or overstressed, then I suggest you think of some other excuse for your behaviour, which is totally unacceptable.'

And on that note she spun on her heel—high, and part of a most attractive golden sandal—and stalked out of the room.

Grant leaned against the sink and stared out the window.

He did try to think of some excuse for his behaviour, but could come up with nothing—apart from temporary insanity. And if he pleaded that, Katie would ban him from seeing patients in case it happened in a doctor-patient situation.

And rightly so.

Though he didn't think it would. The insanity thing seemed to be solely connected to her.

He was still trying to think when she walked back into the kitchen, this time carrying a handbag that matched the cheeky sandals.

'Cassie's down the road at Tara's place, and I'll be back in time to feed her there before afternoon surgery. If you take any emergency calls that come in between now and then, I'll take the surgery, so you'll be free from two until tomorrow morning. I'll leave you the car.'

She was halfway out the kitchen door when he had to ask—just had to.

Though he tried hard to sound casual about it.

'Where are you off to—should I need you?'

He was congratulating himself on injecting just the right degree of nonchalance into the words when she turned, smiled brilliantly at him, then answered.

'I'm having lunch with Brian.'

CHAPTER NINE

HAVING lunch with Brian wasn't quite the 'date' Grant might have been imagining, but it served him right for butting in with remarks about her private life.

Having lunch with Brian, Kate realised, as she trudged uptown towards the bank, was about on a par in the excitement stakes with cleaning the fluff out from under the washing machine. And on top of that, now she was actually on her way, it renewed all the guilty feelings she had about the rift with her mother. Her parents would be only too happy to lend her the money for the renovations—in fact, her father would be hurt if, by chance, her application for a loan came to his attention.

Not that it should—state managers had better things to do than check out small personal loans made in remote country towns.

But if Brian had to get approval from a district manager—who happened to be one of her father's best friends...

Or if her father were to idly flick through a data bank on his computer...

By the time she reached the bank, she was so confused she wondered why she'd ever made the appointment.

'Kate—lovely to see you. And how beautiful you look. Motherhood does suit you. The baby's well?'

Brian always seemed to rush into speech as soon as they met, but today Kate appreciated the verbal outpourings as it gave her time to recover her nerve and steel herself for whatever lie she might have to tell as she persuaded him to keep her request to himself.

'We're both fine,' she replied, smiling at him to make

up for any lack of enthusiasm in her words. 'It's kind of you to make time for me like this.'

This mild appreciation prompted another flood of assurances, delight and confused half-sentences, making Kate wonder if he might be as nervous as she was over the meeting.

He ushered her into his office and shut the door, and, anxious to get the matter out in the open, she came straight to the point.

'I need a loan—a personal loan—for a second bathroom—for a nanny, you see, or visitors, or whatever—and I know you probably have to get approval, but I don't want my father thinking I'm not managing very well should it happen to come to his attention through someone who knows someone. He might also think I'm over-extending myself, and I wondered if there was any way I could get some money that only you know about.'

'Well, I know the bank would approve a small loan through the usual channels, or I could lend it to you myself if you'd like that better,' Brian said. 'We'd do it legally, with signed agreements and all, but I've quite a bit put by, and I'd be happy to do it, Kate. Only too happy. Any time. A private arrangement, no worries, and you needn't think I'd cheat you on interest. I could let you have it interest-free, say, for twelve months, then we could discuss it again.'

Kate felt an enormous weight lift off her shoulders. She could see the bathroom taking shape.

Of course, it would mean Grant shifting into the small bedroom, but he'd said he wouldn't mind, and the baby didn't need it yet. Though having Grant just through one wall instead of two—

'So what about it?'

She stared blankly at Brian. She'd been so lost in her plans for the immediate future she'd totally missed whatever he'd been saying.

'I'm sorry. I was thinking of the bathroom, and phoning Mr McConagle, and all the other things I need to do. Christmas decorations, too.'

Brian looked confused.

'What were you saying?' Kate prompted.

'You haven't said yes or no.'

He was smiling at her, and suddenly Grant's words about marrying Brian came rushing back to her. Had she been wrong thinking Brian's friendship had stemmed from his anxiety to be nice to the big boss's daughter?

And if it *was* more than that, then accepting his offer would almost certainly be wrong because it might give him the wrong idea.

But it *would* solve all her problems!

'I'm sorry.' She offered a smile of her own. 'I guess I didn't think it would be so easy. I need to think about it—about which way to go.'

She was stumbling over the words, anxious not to hurt him, wanting to avoid conflict with her father, but uncertain of the ramifications of borrowing privately, so when he spoke again she was still weighing up the pros and cons—or trying to ignore the cons.

'I wondered if you'd like to come to the bank's Christmas party on Saturday night,' he said. 'It's a dinner-dance at the Commercial Hotel, for the staff and their families and some of our larger accounts. That country and western band from Craigtown's doing the music.'

Pleased to have something easy to answer, Kate rushed in.

'That would be wonderful—I really need to get out and meet more people in the town—as people rather than patients—but I can't promise, of course. I had suggested to Grant that he take the weekend off, so I'd be on call.'

Brian looked so disappointed she rushed to reassure him.

'Not that I'd be likely to be called out.'

He beamed at her, told her he'd look forward to hearing

from her about the loan and would draw up two sets of papers ready for her signature so, whatever she decided, the loan wouldn't be delayed.

'And now the business is done, let's have lunch. I asked the Star Café to send in sandwiches. I hope that's OK.'

His nervousness prompted her to overreact again, assuring and reassuring while wondering how someone who always seemed so ill-at-ease could handle his responsible job, but as they ate he chatted on about the district, seemingly more relaxed when not in bank manager mode.

Kate glanced at her watch before she left the bank. Not enough time to buy Christmas decorations before collecting Cassie from Tara and getting to work.

She walked with long, swift strides, pleased the loan could be organised though not sure which way she'd go. A personal loan would solve so many problems—but would it lead to more? Probably! She'd think about other things—the alterations and the baby—think about anything that would take her mind off personal loans and, more particularly, off Grant Bell—off the feel of his lips on hers, off the hardness of his body as she'd pressed against it.

'Such a happy lunch with Brian you're still smiling?'

It was as if her thoughts had conjured him up, but when she recovered from the shock of Grant's sudden appearance and looked around, she realised he'd come out of the bakery.

'Yes! In fact, it was such a happy lunch I might be smiling for a couple of weeks,' she told him. 'Have you been reminiscing with Codger?'

'Trying his pies. They're not bad.'

Grant spoke lightly, but no smile accompanied the words. Kate glanced towards him and caught the faint markings of a frown lingering between his eyebrows.

'Not good either?' she asked, then added, 'Codger's pies,' when he looked confusedly at her.

'I don't know what you're talking about.' He spoke so

crossly Kate let the subject drop, though even walking with Grant, his steps fitting hers, his body so close, was filling her head with all the things it shouldn't think, and tantalising her nerve endings with a fuzzy kind of excitement that was dangerous in the extreme.

Talking would be much better.

'Brian's willing to lend me the money for the renovations.' It was the first thing that popped into her head. 'So I can phone Mr McConagle from work and let him know to start.'

They'd reached Tara's house and she opened the gate then turned back to Grant.

'Isn't it exciting?'

Definite frown this time.

'You mean the bank's lending you the money?' he growled as Tara appeared, Cassie in her arms.

'I was just going to give her a bottle, but saw you walking down the street and thought she could wait. If you're on your way to work, do you want to feed her here rather than go home?'

'Thanks, Tara, it would certainly save a little time.'

Kate glanced towards Grant, who was still standing on the footpath outside Tara's front gate.

Frowning.

'I'll see you later,' she said, aware she hadn't answered his question and wondering about her reluctance to do so.

Because he'd put into words her own doubts or because it was none of his business?

He nodded, but in such a way she knew he was aware of the omission.

And, no doubt, intended to rectify it.

It was none of his damn business where she got her money, Grant told himself as he walked back to the house.

Neither was being one room closer to her any different from where he'd been, he assured himself as he packed his extremely limited wardrobe and shifted into the smaller bedroom.

But whether it was proximity, or the nanny thing, or the thought of 'Brian' lending her money, not even a ride on his bike, a quiet ride past gum-shrouded waterholes and wide grassy plains stretching to the rugged mountains so familiar from his childhood, could lift the black mood that enveloped him.

Katie came home as he was stripping off his leathers.

'I hope you haven't been speeding. It's bad enough you ride one of those death machines, without taking risks by going too fast.'

He turned towards her. She was still glowing—he hoped it was the yellow top, not Brian, prompting the inner light—and Cassie rested easily in one arm. Which should have stopped, not increased the rush of physical attraction that tightened every sinew in his body.

'And what business is it of yours?' he growled, and felt a spurt of satisfaction when she started at his tone.

'I need a locum, that's what business it is of mine,' she snapped, recovering far too well. 'At least until I get a second bathroom and a nanny.'

'After which, as far as I'm concerned, I can kill myself on my bike?' He spoke without thinking, giving way to some of the venom poisoning his blood.

She went so white he thought she'd faint, and he reached out automatically to grab hold of her. But she shook him off, glared at him, then said, 'Don't you *ever* say things like that, Grant Bell. Don't you ever even *think* things like that!'

Then, clutching Cassie more tightly to her chest, she walked away, leaving Grant more shaken by her reaction—and his own reaction to her reaction—than by the words. Pulling his leathers back on and going for another ride wasn't an option, though it was the most appealing idea.

He decided it must have been a momentary shock, perhaps to do with the fact she'd had the baby in her arms when she'd looked as if she'd faint, that had made his heart squeeze so hard it had hurt him. It had been a protection reflex, that's all, and protection was a normal male reaction—to protect and procreate, weren't they the basic reasons for men's existence in the scheme of things?

He wouldn't think about the procreating now, though certain aspects of it were never far from his mind these days. And he'd accept that the protection thing was simply instinctive—nothing to do with the fact that it was Katie who'd turned so white.

Though he'd better check she was OK.

He walked into the house, still confused, and found her, whatever she might have felt apparently forgotten, smiling as she chatted with Mr McConagle on the phone.

Which reminded him of the loan—and the question she hadn't answered earlier.

Aware that it was none of his business, but needing to know nonetheless, he waited until she finished the call then tried a casual approach.

'So, you got a bank loan for the extensions. Well done. Would you like a drink to celebrate? A small glass of white wine shouldn't bother Cassie.'

He opened the fridge as he spoke, and pulled out the bottle of wine he'd bought earlier, then, aware of the silence descending on the room, turned to look at her.

At pinkness in her cheeks?

'What's wrong? What did you have to do? Have sex with him in the office?'

His voice, which had started as a low growl, grew harsher as imagination raised the level of his anger.

The pinkness turned to the red of rage and she stood up and stepped towards him, her arm lifting ready to swing towards his face.

He caught her wrist in time to stop the slap, but couldn't stop the flow of words.

'How dare you talk to me that way? How dare you even suggest such a thing? What's wrong with you, Grant? What's got you so screwed up your mind would even think of something like that?'

He heard the rage in her voice, but his own had gone way beyond the point of no return. Still holding her wrist gave him the power to draw her towards him.

With her face no more than six inches from his own, he answered.

'I'll tell you what's got into me, Katie Fenton. You have. You and your short shorts and long legs and your tangled, sexy-as-hell hair, and living in the same house, seeing you, smelling you, sensing your presence in the air. It's driving me to distraction—but it would only be sex, and I'd still be moving on, so in fairness to you I'm fighting it. Understand?'

Huge bewildered green eyes looked appealingly into his, and resolve, accompanied by good intentions, flew out the window.

'But I can only take so much!' he muttered, then he bent and claimed her softly parted lips, sealing whatever she might have been about to say with a kiss so hot and needy he felt her gasp before her body slumped against his and she slipped her wrist out of his grasp so she could reach for his shoulders to steady herself while she kissed him back.

He was aware of her softness, so different to the angular Katie he'd known, but the passion with which she responded was exactly how he remembered it, and the way it fed his own desire, like fierce winds fanning bush fires, reminded him of those wild encounters by the river.

When they stopped for air, and because he had to stop right then or carry her off to the bedroom to finish what he'd never intended starting, he had to steady her with his hands on her shoulders and ignore the silent appeal in those so expressive eyes.

Then she breathed deeply and put it into words.

'I could probably do with some sex. It's been a long time and it was never much fun with Mark.'

She spoke like someone in a dream, then shook her head and stepped away from him.

'Though I wouldn't ever do that to another woman—help her man to cheat. I couldn't do that to Linda.'

Grant was so busy assimilating Katie's bold confession about the sex that it took a while to work out who Linda was and why she'd entered the conversation. And by that time Katie was prattling on about Mr McConagle starting the following day and would Grant mind doing the morning session again as she had to sign Brian's loan papers at the bank?

A jolt, different from the one he'd felt earlier but just as strong, all but rattled his bones.

'Brian's loan? You mean the bank's loan.'

The pinkness that had started all of this returned to her cheeks, but this time it was accompanied by a defiant tilt of her slightly pointed chin.

'No, I mean Brian's loan. It's a personal arrangement.'

'But you can't borrow money from him,' Grant protested. 'It puts you under an obligation and, given the way he feels about you...'

Oops. Foot in mouth again—in fact, so far in it was probably lodged in his chest.

Katie's eyes glittered dangerously, but her voice, when she spoke, was very soft.

'And what business of yours is it? Whatever Brian does or doesn't feel about me has nothing whatsoever to do with you!'

She stalked away before he could find an answer, though she obviously wouldn't have listened even if he'd thought of something to say.

Damn it all! As she'd told him earlier, it was none of his business what she did and the sooner he got that into his thick skull, the sooner they could get things back onto a friendly footing.

Friendly footing? Hollow laughter sounded in his head. As if such a thing would be possible after that last kiss.

His body tightened at the memory then became more aroused as he remembered her admission that she wanted sex as much as he did.

Though she hadn't stipulated him as a partner...

And Brian was lending her money...

Desire ebbed away.

Kate's fury took her as far as the bedroom. She was aware she'd made things worse by pretending she'd already decided to accept Brian's offer—and needling Grant with the pretence—but she'd been so confused by the kiss...

Fury gave way to guilt, only this time it wasn't the guilt she'd felt when she'd realised how much she wanted to take Grant's kisses further—when she knew full well he was engaged to another woman—but guilt that she could bring her anger so close to her child.

'Sorry, little one,' she said, peering into the crib and feeling relief that the baby slept on, apparently unaware of the tension Kate assumed had been radiating from her body.

She slumped onto the bed and stared at the ceiling. It was her turn to cook dinner—steak and salad—and she should be in the kitchen, putting bits of lettuce in a salad bowl and chopping things to make the lettuce more interesting. But as her anger had eased, then been deliberately doused in the bedroom, an uncertainty had risen at the other end of her see-sawing emotions.

Was she wrong to borrow money from Brian? *Would* it put her under an obligation to him?

Yes, and yes, the stern internal killjoy said, in answer to these questions.

Maybe she shouldn't have agreed to go to the dinner-dance...

Though she *was* a bank customer, and if the bank was lending her money it should be OK.

Though the personal loan was still tempting...

No!

A light tap on the door startled her awake.

'Katie! Are you there? Dinner's ready.'

She leapt from the bed, horrified she'd been asleep, and raced to open the door.

'It was my turn,' she told Grant, who was hovering uncertainly in the hall. 'I'm sorry! I must have fallen asleep.'

His lips eased into the grin that made her bones melt, even though she'd now remembered she was furious with him.

'You probably needed it. And I had nothing to do, so it was no bother.'

He walked away, but not before she'd read confusion in his eyes.

Confused *and* uncertain?

Get real, Kate! She *had* to be imagining it.

But her own uncertainty had her hesitating now. She checked the baby, went through to the bathroom to drag a comb through her unruly hair and straighten the now crumpled skirt and top.

Perhaps she should change.

'Come on, Katie. The steaks will go from medium to well done to charcoal if you don't come now.'

Unable to dither any longer, she walked through to the kitchen where they ate all their meals. A spray of bougainvillaea rested in the centre of the table, place-mats were neatly aligned opposite each other and the presence of both wine and water glasses suggested there'd be another offer of a celebratory drink.

Was it an apology?

'I made a Caesar salad and a potato salad, so help yourself while I whack the steaks onto a serving dish.'

It sounded like an apology—of sorts!

Kate helped herself to healthy portions of each of the salads, then held out her plate for the steak he was offering. Once again he smiled, this time as he slid the piece of meat onto the plate, but the blue eyes when they looked at her were still clouded with some emotion she didn't understand.

Though lack of understanding didn't stop the rush of longing that flooded through her body, a longing she recognised not as lust but love—love and the pain it brought in its train when the loved one was hurting.

He has a fiancée, and a city career awaiting him, and has told you all he wants from you is sex, so forget it, Kate.

The stern admonition had so little effect she might as well have saved her brain cells for working out how to combat the implications of this new revelation.

'Eat!'

The order came so abruptly she glanced up, and once again the blue eyes were her undoing. Scrabbling around in her head for something to discuss before she blurted out how she was feeling, she remembered where the argument and kiss business had begun.

'I considered getting a loan from Brian and not the bank because I really didn't want it to get back to Dad. Although I know it's unlikely it would, stranger things have happened. They'll be coming for a visit as soon as they get home and I don't want Dad spending the whole time lecturing me on keeping within my means.'

The words came out in a rush, but didn't seem to appease her companion. Far from understanding, he looked even more annoyed than he had when she'd first mentioned Brian earlier.

'What about credit cards and overdraft facilities? As a bank manager he could have increased your limit on those without anyone else being any the wiser.'

Kate contemplated this statement, and felt the frown

puckering her brow. Although she'd nearly—well, almost certainly—decided not to get the loan from Brian, she still couldn't fathom Grant's interest.

Or his reaction.

'But credit-card rates are really high, and I've already got an overdraft—that's how I bought the house and practice. What's so wrong with borrowing from Brian?'

She didn't add, 'from your point of view', though that's what she meant, as she knew her own reservations.

Grant's frown looked far more ferocious than her own felt.

'Because it puts you under an obligation—it's not as if you know him well.'

'Of course I know him well. He's been a good friend to me since I came to Testament. He mows my lawn.'

'Mowed your lawn,' Grant corrected, still frowning. 'And I thought I was a friend as well. Why not borrow from me?'

Kate cut a piece of steak, lifted it to her mouth and chewed carefully. She had about forty easy answers to Grant's question. Why should I? I didn't think of it. What would Linda think? Those were only three of them, but she had a feeling that, while the loan might be the obvious topic of conversation, there were undercurrents to it she didn't understand.

But were they dangerous enough to sweep her away?

The idea was weird enough to ignore but the feeling too strong for her to banish completely, so she kept quiet about the second loan offer and pursued the matter—but trod carefully.

'I intended getting it from the bank, but when I mentioned doing it quietly, Brian came up with the offer. It's no big deal, Grant.'

It wasn't, of course. Grant knew that, though he couldn't bring himself to admit it to Katie.

Neither could he understand how screwed up it made him feel inside.

'Well, as long as you don't feel under any obligation,' he managed to reply, hoping his voice didn't sound quite as growly to Katie as it did in his own ears. Then, just as things might have settled back onto an even keel, some malign fate reminded him of the remark Katie had made earlier. 'I could do with some sex,' she'd said.

'In any way!' he added, not even attempting to hide the growl. 'And you know what I mean! You've admitted to having sexual needs, and he's been kind, and gratitude can be mistaken for other emotions and then you'll end up in a tangle.'

'You mean in his bed!' Katie said, icy disdain sharpening her voice to razor-like proportions. 'And you wanting to have sex with me while engaged to Linda isn't getting you into a tangle?' Kate's green eyes glittered with something he didn't quite understand. 'I'll admit I hadn't quite thought of Brian that way,' she continued, as cool as the ice in her voice, 'but, now you mention it, he does have a good body and, yes, I'm a woman and I do have sexual needs, so maybe Saturday night, after the dinner-dance—'

'You're going out with him? See, it's the obligation thing already. And having sex with a man because he has a good body is the most irresponsible thing I've ever heard of.' Grant was on his feet, leaning across the table, wanting to grab her shoulders and shake her to make her understand. But the eyes that met his were now easy to read—they glowed with an anger so hot he wondered it wasn't scorching his skin.

'Are you suggesting that me having sex with someone with a bad body would be more acceptable?'

Grant slumped back into his chair and pushed his half-finished dinner away.

'I'm not suggesting any such thing, Katie Fenton, and you bloody well know it.' He searched for something else to say—something to make things at least part-way right between them again. 'But you've Cassie to consider, and small-town gossip, and how that might affect her later on.'

'Are you saying I should keep myself pure but frustrated, so Cassie doesn't have kids whispering about her mother when she goes to school? For how long? Five years? Or eighteen, until she leaves home, when I can then have sex with every man in town?'

He could hear the quiver in her voice, and see the strength of her emotions in the trembling of her fingers. Devastated that he'd made such a total hash of things, he reached across the table and took her hand.

'I'm sorry, Katie. I was way out of line. But I want so much for you to be happy, and for you and Cassie to have a wonderful and fulfilling life. And if that means having a man in your life, I hope you find one who truly loves and appreciates you.' The words nearly choked him, but he got them said so he could add the rider. 'But take your time. Don't fall into bed with the first man who comes along. Guard your emotions so you don't get hurt again.'

Too late for that warning, Kate thought, but her hand felt so warm and right in Grant's she let it stay there.

And she found a smile to offer him in return for the comfort of those long, strong fingers.

'Isn't that a bit defeatist, Dr Bell? Especially coming from the lips of a prime risk-taker like yourself? And leaving Mark, when the time came, didn't hurt. In fact, it was the easiest of partings, because I knew it was right for me.'

His thumb was rubbing the back of her forefinger and, though she'd never considered that bit of skin as part of any erogenous zone, the movement was sending startlingly explicit messages through her body.

She should remove her hand.

Now!

But he probably didn't even realise he was doing it—

and certainly wouldn't in his wildest dreams have guessed what it was doing to her.

So to withdraw her hand might seem…unfriendly?

She turned her attention to his face, and found him smiling at her—with eyes as well as lips this time.

'I can't imagine you admitting if it had hurt, Katie,' he said gently. 'You might have railed against what you saw as injustice, or taken up a fight on behalf of someone else, but I never heard you complain about your own lot, or saw you cry over an injury.'

'Until the week you arrived, when all I seemed to do was weep. It's a wonder you didn't turn around and go straight back to Byron Bay.'

His grip tightened on her fingers, sending more tremors through her body.

'Maybe it would have been better if I had,' he said quietly, then he released her hand, stood up, tipped his dinner into the trash can and dumped the plate in the sink.

'I'm going out,' he said. 'Leave the dishes and I'll do them later.'

'Nonsense—I'll do them,' Kate told him, surprised she'd managed to form the words when she was breathless with fear for him. Then, much as she tried not to say it, she couldn't hold back the words. 'N-not on your bike? You won't ride your bike?'

Grant was at the back door as she stammered out the feeble pleas, and turned, frowning again.

'I'm only going over to Vi's,' he said. 'On foot!'

And though her panic eased on that count, another worry arose to confront her.

The 'maybe it would have been better if I had' statement he'd made before his precipitate departure.

CHAPTER TEN

It was nonsense, Kate assured herself, but the sick feeling in her stomach and the dull ache in the region of her heart suggested it probably *would* have been better if Grant had gone straight back—or if he'd never come.

She thought back to the strange conversation that had preceded his departure—to her rage over his reaction to her innocent acceptance of Brian's invitation to the bank's Christmas party. She'd stood up for herself then, flinging stupid words at him as her temper had flared, but that's all they'd been—words. In truth, when she'd decided to go ahead with her pregnancy and had planned her life—hers and Cassie's—she'd never for a moment considered a relationship with another man somewhere further down the track. In her relief to be free of Mark and the emptiness of what they'd shared, the single state had seemed to offer everything she'd ever need.

Until Grant Bell had come back into her life, reawakening not only the heat and longing of desire with an intensity she'd thought she'd never feel again but, worse, reminding her of the ease with which she could talk to him, the special bond she'd always felt in his presence, the sense of completeness he'd brought to her life—so many years ago.

Yes, maybe it would have been better if he had, as he'd murmured, gone straight back to Byron Bay.

Though she certainly wouldn't have managed without him.

The sharp summons of the phone brought her out of the useless cogitation, and the emergency, a child who'd swallowed half a bottle of cranberry capsules because they'd looked pretty, had her on the phone to Tara, then hot-footing it across to the hospital.

'They probably won't do any harm,' she assured the panicking parents, 'but we'll try to get rid of them anyway.'

She was examining little Richie Webb as she spoke, talking quietly to him, asking how he felt.

The four-year-old was alert—perhaps too alert, though he was always an active child, and his respiration and pulse were normal.

'Rather than intubating him to use a stomach pump, I'd rather try an emetic—something to make him sick,' she told Mrs Webb. 'It's less traumatic than the stomach pump.'

The anxious mother nodded, and Kate explained to Richie that he'd have to have a drink and it might make him sick.

'But being sick is good because it will get all those silly tablets out of your tummy.'

The little boy nodded, and Narelle, again on duty, hurried off to get a basin, while Kate measured out two teaspoons of syrup of ipecac for the little boy.

'Just drink this down, Richie, then I'll give you a glass of water.'

She glanced up at his parents.

'Be prepared for a fast reaction, though if it doesn't work within thirty minutes I can give him another dose.'

The second dose wasn't needed, and the fourteen tablets, still encased in their gel coating, were safely remitted.

Leaving Richie resting on a table in the emergency room, Kate took the empty bottle of cranberry tablets and hurried through to her office. As the capsules still looked intact, there was a chance none of the constituents had entered Richie's stomach, but she'd have to check the list of ingredients against known contraindications before giving him activated charcoal as a precautionary measure.

She explained this to Mr and Mrs Webb when she returned minutes later.

'So, just in case some bad stuff got out of the tablets and into your tummy, Richie,' she told the little boy, 'I want you to take this tablet. You know how Mummy's sponge picks up spills in the kitchen? Well, that's what this tablet will do in your tummy. It will pick up any bad stuff left and you'll be OK.'

'Will I have to be sick again?' he demanded, giving Kate a look that suggested he'd rather be poisoned.

'No, not this time,' she assured him.

'Then where will it go?'

His clear, pale blue eyes challenged her and, with his parents exchanging amused glances, Kate grabbed a diagram of the alimentary canal and proceeded to explain just how it worked, in simple enough terms for a four-year-old to understand.

Richie's main delight was in the end result.

'He's at an age when "bottom" is the funniest word he knows and anything to do with bodily functions is a cause of great interest,' Mr Webb explained.

Kate nodded, knowing children of friends who hooted with laughter over the same word, and whispered behind their hands about the less attractive features of the end product of their alimentary canals. Then, while Richie regaled Narelle with some of the things his friends said at preschool, Kate spoke to his parents about precautions they might take in future.

'I do know all that,' Mrs Webb said earnestly. 'We've a child-proof lock on the cupboard under the sink where I keep cleaning things, and Jeff has a lock on the garden shed. But my grandmother's staying with us, and she takes the cranberry, and heaven knows what else. Richie must have slipped into her bedroom while we were having dinner, and it wasn't until Grandma was going to bed that she realised the tablets were missing.'

'You can't be on guard all the time,' Kate assured her. 'And there's no harm done. A good night's sleep and he'll be back to normal. Although if he does seem unusually quiet or if you're worried about him in any way, don't hesitate to call me.'

Both parents thanked her, then Mr Webb lifted their son into his arms and carried him out to the car.

How long would she be able to lift Cassie? Kate wondered. Until she was five—six?

She scuffed her feet against the path as she walked home, concerned because the spectre of bringing up a child alone was once again a pressing concern on her shoulders.

Smiled to herself, because Grant had been so reassuring whenever she'd expressed the stupid fears that beset her so regularly. Then she remembered how they'd parted, and stopped smiling.

He was going, anyway, and she'd have to manage on her own—as she'd always intended.

But thoughts of Grant lingered in her mind, and after paying Tara and seeing her safely on her way home, she walked through the house, knowing he wasn't there but looking for him anyway. His bedroom door was open but the room was empty. Not only emptied of his possessions, but totally emptied. He must have shifted things while she'd been at work.

She walked to the next door—which was pulled close but not shut—and tapped before pushing it open. The bed with flowered sheets had been moved in and pushed against the other single to form a larger bed. She should have done that earlier, for someone as tall as Grant. The chest of drawers from the bigger bedroom was tucked behind the sliding doors of the built-in wardrobe where there was plenty of room, given Grant's lack of clothes.

Kate sniffed the air, already masculine though he'd barely used it, then she saw the briefcase on top of the dressing-table.

'My papers are in my briefcase in my room if you'd care to look.'

She recalled the words he'd said that first day, before going out to see George Barrett.

She'd never looked, and although, tonight, it seemed like an invasion of privacy, she assured herself it was a responsible thing to do. A little late, admittedly, but still responsible!

She carried the worn leather case to the bed, rubbing her fingers on the leather because she knew his fingers had touched it. Telling herself not to be pathetic but doing it anyway.

Opening the clasp, she leafed through the manilla folders it held. New appointment letter—she'd like to look at that but had no right. Personal. Nothing to do with her. Definitely nothing to do with her. Bills—well, that one she didn't want. CV. That was it.

She pulled it out and opened it, laying it flat on the bed. Read through his school results—Miss Jones's mammary glands couldn't have had all that damaging an effect, from the results he'd got in final year maths. Results Kate hadn't known because he'd been gone before they'd been published.

She flipped over pages, trying not to think of that summer, and came to the précis of his medical career. University of New South Wales, then North Shore Hospital, followed by A and E at St George for three years.

Making money to buy back the farm, until he'd become an adrenalin junkie and had decided he liked it. Recalling his words, she studied the time frame once again. Three years and two months. Not a contract, then, in that fourth year. Contracts were usually longer—three months minimum. It looked more as if something had happened.

She went on to the next line. GP training—big switch. Perhaps he'd been waiting for a training position in a general practice and had continued in A and E until one came up. She checked the dates but they didn't fit—there was a four-month gap between when he left A and E and when he took up his post at the practice. Perhaps he'd been overseas, though leafing through the folder gave no indication of any overseas experience or study.

'It was a holiday—after three years and two months in A and E he'd have needed one.'

She spoke out loud, hoping to convince herself, but the words didn't have any more effect when heard aloud than when she'd thought them.

Kate turned a page. Twelve months' training, then GP work for eleven months, then another sudden switch—back to a lowly resident in paediatrics.

Two years there—not so lowly second year—took her up to two weeks before he'd appeared on her veranda with his 'knight in shining armour' routine. And the new job was in a training post for paediatric oncology—he'd told her that—a follow-on from what he'd been doing.

She was puzzling over the shifts and possible reasons for them when she heard Grant's footsteps entering the kitchen. Not wanting to appear furtive, she remained where she was, the papers spread in front of her, and when he entered the room she gave him what she hoped wasn't a furtive smile.

'You did tell me to check your credentials. I just never got around to it.'

He remained where he was, just inside the door, looking at her in a way she couldn't read.

'You stopped and started at odd times, and the gap after you left A and E—did you go overseas?'

He didn't answer, though his eyes remained fixed on her—or were they on her? She couldn't be sure, but what she did know was that some new tension had entered the room—not with him, but emanating from him now.

'I'm sorry. I should have asked first—it was ages ago you said to look.' She gathered up the papers but in her haste knocked the briefcase to the floor so the folders she'd half pulled out spilled to the floor, opening enough for papers to flutter everywhere.

'Oh, I'm sorry. I'll pick them up.'

She reached out, lifted a bundle and was about to shove them back into the closest folder when she saw the photo that lay beneath them. Grant was by her side, so she didn't miss his reaction either, didn't miss the tremor in his hand as he reached out to lift it, moving it out of her grasp—out of her sight.

Instinct made her grasp his wrist and stop him hiding it. Instinct took her further so she knelt closer to him and reached out her free hand to turn his face towards her.

'I guessed a baby, but I don't know any more. You're far better at changing Cassie's nappies than I am—you had to have had experience. Let me see him, Grant. Tell me.'

He didn't answer, neither would he look at her or reveal the image on the photo he held protectively against his chest.

Kate traced the lines that had deepened on his face.

'They're lines of pain—I knew that when you first returned. But wouldn't sharing it help you take the next step to recovery? Isn't there enough of our old friendship left for me to be the one you talk to?'

He lifted his head and what she saw in his blue eyes terrified her. It wasn't grief, but a kind of blankness—like the bewildered terror of a child who'd lost his way.

Kate forgot the photo and wrapped her arms around him, drawing him close and rocking his body against hers.

'Let's forget it for a while. Leave the papers here. Come with me, we can lie on my bed. We don't have to talk but at least I can hold you—we can hold each other. Everyone needs someone to hold occasionally.'

He didn't argue, though he did help her to her feet and allow her arm to stay wrapped around his shoulders as they walked into the bedroom.

Stay asleep, Kate willed the baby as she pulled back the sheet and guided Grant's obviously numbed body down onto the bed. Then she lay beside him and, as promised, held him, resting his head on her shoulder, running her fingers through his hair, stroking his back and kneading at his shoulders.

The words, when they came, were muffled, but though Kate's heart hurt when she heard Debbie's name, when Grant spoke of the casual relationship that had resulted in a pregnancy, she said nothing.

'Debbie wanted to keep working for at least another year—it would have given her the seniority she'd need for future jobs. And though I knew I'd have to give up A and E—the hours were too erratic for a family man—I stayed on until Robbie was born, so I could get some paternity leave and do a lot of the caring for those first three months.'

He paused, and Kate could picture him, though little Robbie would have had more cuddles than the occasionally surreptitious ones she knew Grant gave to Cassie.

'Then I went into a GP practice for training, and Debbie worked part time. My mother minded Robbie in between, and things were fine.'

But not ecstatic from the sound of your voice, Kate thought, then regretted it, as she knew it came from a jealousy she had no right to feel.

'Until he was nine months old, when he became listless, failed to thrive. We took him to doctors and finally to specialists. It was diagnosed as a brain tumour, a glioma, in the brain stem, inoperable and, practically speaking, untreatable. Robbie died six months later. Debbie and I had stayed together until then, but with nothing left to bind us that ended as well.'

The words stopped, and Kate's grip tightened. With tears flowing unchecked from her eyes, she used her hands, and the warmth of her body, to try to offer comfort that could never be put into words. A heaviness in Grant's body told her the telling of Robbie's story had left him exhausted, and when his deep, steady breathing suggested he might sleep for a while, she slipped away, covered him with a light cotton blanket, then lifted Cassie, crib and all, and carried her out of the room.

No good taking her into the small bedroom—Grant would still hear her when he woke.

Kate's heart fluttered as she imagined the agony Cassie's cries must already have caused him—unknowing reminders of his tragedy.

'We'll sleep in the living room,' she told her still sleeping baby. 'You have your crib, I'll take the couch.'

But though Cassie slept, Kate couldn't emulate her, too distressed by Grant's story to turn her mind off the baby he'd called Robbie. And, in spite of the fears that beset her daily about her own small infant, it was for Grant she feared through the dark watches of the night. For the laughing carefree teenager who'd already suffered the loss of his beloved home, then had rebuilt his life, only to be hit by another tragedy.

So many things had fallen into place with the telling of the tale—why he was so determined to do further study, why he'd chosen paediatric oncology, why he was so adamant that he'd be gone in a couple of weeks...

Kate could understand it all, but it didn't make the loneliness it prompted any easier to bear. It was as if she'd secretly—subconsciously—been hoping he would stay— that the fairy story which had begun with her knight's arrival would have a 'happy ever after' ending.

'Which is nothing more than self-pity, so don't go there,' she warned her head. 'Think of Grant instead.'

Kate found herself hoping that Linda was good to him— that she understood his pain and could, in some small way, alleviate it.

Then wishing it was herself, not some unknown woman, who had the right to hold him when the memories crowded in on him and his eyes ached with unshed tears.

Cassie gave a quiet cry, prelude to the demand, and Kate leapt off the couch, then realised she'd forgotten to bring a dry nappy from the bedroom. Were there some still in the dryer? Or was that pack of disposables in the pantry?

She picked up the baby before her cries could bother Grant, dropped a kiss on her head and carried her through to the kitchen. Yes! Disposables. They'd do for one night. She changed Cassie on the kitchen table, marvelling at her growth and beauty, refusing to even contemplate the existence of baby-killing tumours.

'It's so rare, it certainly won't happen to you,' she assured her little one, then she lifted her into her arms and carried her back to the living room. 'Statistically as unlikely as a tourist flight to the moon tomorrow.'

Cassie dropped off to sleep as she finished her meal, and Kate returned her to the crib, then stood, looking down at her. Thinking of another baby, and the aching loss she'd heard in Grant's voice.

She tiptoed to the bedroom door and cracked it open. Grant lay in a tangle of sheets which were becoming even more tangled as he tossed restlessly. The breeze coming through the open door was cooler now, and she moved closer, thinking to straighten the top sheet and cover him as she'd covered her baby.

But he stirred as she tried to unwind the soft cotton material from around his legs and groaned, then shifted restlessly, his hand touching her arm. As if comforted by finding her, finding something to anchor him, he grabbed it and pulled her close, until she found herself nestled up against his body—again!

And thinking things she shouldn't—again!

But Grant needed comfort, someone to hold onto until his dreams and pain subsided. Someone to be there for him in the dark watches of the night, when the death of his baby boy returned to haunt him.

OK, so she wasn't the right someone but she was the only person available. And she loved him—there, she'd admitted it, so the least she could do was be there for him just this once.

She banished confused and confusing thoughts to concentrate on Grant—and his need—tonight. And moved closer so her body fitted itself to his, and she could hold him.

Grant knew it had to be a dream—it wasn't the first. He'd had one just like it since he arrived back in Testament. But this time Katie felt real, and her sweet, soft body was snuggled up against him, as if this was where she was meant to be.

And if she was meant to be here, he could kiss her neck like this, and nuzzle that place below her ear where he'd discovered sensitive skin so long ago. And the buttons on the shirt she wore to bed seemed to have come undone, so he could touch her breasts, hold the heaviness, tease the nipple so she'd make the funny little noise of wanting only Katie had ever made.

So he kissed her, and it certainly didn't feel like a dream. Surely in the dreams she hadn't kissed him back.

Fuzzily, he began to remember—Katie on his bed, the papers dropping, Robbie's photo.

More recollection—this was Katie's bed, and Katie's body stretched beside him.

No! She'd left earlier—it *had* to be a dream.

And if it wasn't a dream, it was a disaster, for if there was one thing he knew above all others, he was only seconds away from making love to Katie Fenton. And leaving Katie Fenton—hard though it was going to be anyway—after making love to her would be well nigh impossible.

She was touching him, unbuttoning his shirt, running her fingers through the fine swirl of hair on his chest, sliding her hands lower...

But Cassie came with Katie, and he was already halfway to loving the tiny baby.

He tried to analyse the situation more rationally but the

tight buds of her nipples brushing across his chest suggested she was as aroused as she must surely know he was.

Was she here because she felt sorry for him?

The thought was abhorrent, but he'd better mention it—just in case.

'I don't want pity, Katie.'

Damn! He hadn't meant to say it that way, but it came out harshly enough for her to recoil, but, like Katie of old, she didn't go far, standing up to his challenge with all her old defiance.

'I am not offering you pity, Grant Bell, I'm offering you comfort, and if comfort includes sex, well, that's on offer, too—just for tonight—because of Robbie.'

She'd sat up so he could see the upper half of her body silhouetted against the light from the veranda doors.

'And if you're worried about Linda, then so am I, but if she never knows than it can't hurt her…'

Already confused by emotion, arousal and the still clinging remnants of sleep, the mention of some unknown woman's name tipped Grant's mind into total bewilderment.

'Who the hell is Linda?' he demanded, and felt, rather than saw, Katie recoil. She was out of the bed in a flash, positively gasping with whatever emotion his seemingly innocent remark had generated.

'And to think I felt sorry for you!' she snapped, snatching the sheet off the bed so swiftly she almost tugged him out as well, then holding it to her scantily clad body as she stalked out of the room.

'Then it *was* pity,' Grant snapped right back, but she was already gone and if she heard, she didn't answer.

'Damn and blast all women to hell!' he muttered to himself as he sank back against the pillow. He'd remembered Linda now, but what he remembered far more clearly—far too clearly—was the feel of Katie's body snuggled up to his, the ripples of sensory excitement in his skin as her heavy breasts had brushed across his chest.

His head ached, probably from the telling of Robbie's story, which always brought with it such a burden of defeat. His desire refused to subside, so he was feeling pain down there as well, and his mind had ceased to function so he couldn't work out where to go from here—what to do or say to make things right again.

Eventually he slept, but not before he'd heard Cassie cry and felt the familiar spurt of tension and remembrance the sound always caused.

Kate was in the kitchen, precautionary tales about drinking coffee while breastfeeding set aside as she gulped down a strong black brew. After a totally sleepless night, she needed something before she faced Mr McConagle.

It wouldn't help with facing Grant, of course. Cyanide might, but she didn't have any on hand and, anyway, it wouldn't be right to leave Cassie an orphan.

The thought of her baby made her shiver. What had happened to all her good intentions—her determination to be the best possible mother for her daughter? Was nestling up to Grant in bed the way a responsible mother should behave?

Of course it wasn't.

And as for him—and his 'Who's Linda?'.

What kind of man forgot his own fiancée's name?

She was mulling over whether she was more angry with herself or Grant when the phone rang.

'School bus accident at Four Mile Creek and the ambulance has taken Mrs Stubbs to Craigtown. I'm on my way. Can you come?'

Kate recognised the voice of Dick Harris, the police sergeant, and wasted no time assuring him she'd be there. As she dialled Tara's number, Mr McConagle knocked and came through the back door.

'Could you wake Grant and tell him he's needed?' she said to the handyman, then explained to Tara's mother what was happening. 'So could you send Tara over?' she said into the phone. 'Cassie's not long been fed, and there's boiled water in the fridge if she's desperate before I get back.'

Grant appeared as she put down the receiver, Mr McConagle following.

Kate explained briefly, asked Mr McConagle to mind the baby until Tara arrived and to let Vi know what was happening, then she led Grant out to the car.

'Did Dick say how bad it was?' he asked, steering her towards the passenger seat as he added, 'I'll drive.'

'No, just that he needed us. It's at the Four Mile.'

They drove swiftly and in silence until they were several kilometres from town when Kate saw emus stalking long-leggedly towards the road.

'Emus,' she warned, though she knew Grant had probably seen them, the silly birds racing along the verge as if in competition with the car.

Grant slowed, but couldn't stop to see which way they might dodge as the thought of injured children was in the forefront of both their minds.

The birds, six in all, veered away, then suddenly one skittered back towards the car in a wild, suicidal dance.

'Damn!' Grant muttered, as the bird brushed into the side of the car. 'Silly bloody thing!'

'It's probably all right,' Kate told him, but her assurance didn't soften the grim set of his lips. Remembering the emotional toll his telling of Robbie's story must have had on him the previous evening, she understood an injury to the bird would take on extra significance. Hoping, needing to offer comfort, in spite of where that need had led last night, she rested her hand on his thigh and kneaded it gently.

The flashing lights on the top of the police car, and beyond that the red bulk of the fire engine, told them the crash scene had come into view, and the bus, tipped sideways into a ditch, told its own story. As Grant pulled up behind the police car, Kate grabbed her bag and leapt out.

'We've got all but three of the kids out, and the driver's also trapped,' Dick told her, motioning to where volunteers, who'd apparently appeared from nowhere on the isolated country road, were comforting a group of resting children. 'The firemen are using cutting tools.'

'I'd better go in and see if anyone needs stabilising before he or she is moved,' Kate said, putting down her bag and moving towards the bus.

Grant grabbed her arm.

'Don't be stupid! You check the ones who are out—I'll go in there.'

She twisted out of his grip, and kept going.

'Look at the bus—you'd never get in there. I'm smaller, I'll go. You see to the others.'

For a moment she thought he'd argue, then he nodded and turned away, picking up her bag as he strode towards the huddle of children.

Kate squeezed through the emergency exit window at the back of the bus and crawled along the passage between twisted metal bars and vinyl seating. Ahead of her, a firebrigade volunteer was using heavy pincers to cut metal away from a small boy, and farther towards the front another child whimpered.

'A couple of our chaps are cutting towards the driver from the front, and once they get him out, we should be able to get the two kids from the seat behind him. This one's legs are caught beneath their seat. He's unconscious but he's breathing and there's no obvious blood loss.'

Kate reached around the man, feeling for the child's wrist, feeling the rapid flutter of his pulse. Something grasped her arm and she saw blood on the small fingers. From where she was she couldn't see the child but, knowing he or she was conscious, she knew she had to get closer, if only for reassurance.

She gave the fingers a reassuring squeeze, then said, 'I'm coming, darling. I'll stay with you.'

'Can you let me past?' she asked the man, whom she now recognised as Richie Webb's father.

He wriggled closer to the seat and she squirmed past him, managing to turn so she could face the seat where the other two children were trapped. Outside, the wail of approaching sirens announced that at least one ambulance was finally arriving. Grant would get some help.

From where she was it became obvious the bus had rolled before coming to rest on its side, and the roof had caved in more seriously here in the front section. The trapped driver was hidden from her view by the back of his high seat, and the two children were wedged between it and their own seat, which had been squashed almost flat by the roof.

She pushed her hand towards what she could see of school uniform, felt the rounded leg beneath material, felt warmth and no wetness, and prayed the little one still lived. Then she edged closer into the narrow space and pushed her hand farther, finally encountering the arm of the second child. Once again small fingers found her arm, and then her hand, and, knowing there was nothing she could do until the driver was released, she held the little hand and talked about the day outside, the blue sky they would soon see when the roof was lifted off the bus.

The raw screeching of the power tools cutting into metal set her teeth on edge, and tightened the child's grip on her hand.

'It's just a saw—probably your dad has one,' she said, while behind her she heard Mr Webb grunt in exultation as the metal he was cutting finally gave way.

'I can lift this one backwards now,' he said to Kate. 'Will you come out and check him?'

'Dr Bell's out there, but can you lift him, seat and all? Perhaps just drag the seat backwards and wait until the roof comes off so he can be checked before he's moved. If he has spinal injuries, the seat will protect him. Do you need a hand?'

'No, you stay there,' the man said. 'The roof's moving so they must be close to lifting it. I heard Bob Willis's crane arrive. It should be able to peel the top back as easy as opening a sardine cane.'

'There are some similarities,' Kate commented, then she felt the movement as well and a sudden rush of air as the roof was lifted and blue sky appeared above them.

Also Grant Bell. He glanced her way, nodded as if assuring himself she was OK, then turned his attention to the driver. An ambulance officer handed Grant a neck collar, then a short backboard, which Grant slid between the back of the seat and the driver's body. Straps fastened around his chest and legs fashioned the board into a sling, and men with gentle hands lifted the injured man from his seat.

Within minutes the seat was also removed, allowing Kate her first glimpse of the two children behind it. The owner of the hand, a girl of about seven, smiled at her, but the lad beside her— 'He's my brother, he's asleep' —didn't move.

Then Grant was there, helping Kate to her feet, then strapping a neck and back brace onto the girl before lifting her in his strong arms and stepping out of the bus to pass her to rescuers. Kate bent to examine the boy. His pulse was strong, and he was breathing, but a large bruise already darkening the skin behind his left ear suggested the cause of his concussion.

Kate felt his body, seeking blood, then ran her hands over his arms—the left one gashed but not deeply—and down his legs. His right ankle, which had taken the brunt of the driver's seat when it had collapsed backwards, was certainly broken, but there was no other obvious damage.

'You climb out, I'll get him ready to be lifted.'

Grant was back, his hands on Kate's waist, ready to lift her out as well.

'I can manage,' she told him, but he took no notice, and one look at the determination in his eyes warned her not to argue. Firm, warm, safe hands lifted her onto the outside of the bus where others helped her to the ground.

She crossed to the ambulance where the little girl was being treated, a catheter already inserted into her arm and a drip about to be attached.

'Where's Robbie?' she asked, and Kate, though momentarily taken aback, quickly realised she must be talking about her brother.

'The other doctor is bringing him out now,' Kate said, brushing chips of safety glass out of the child's tangled hair.

'Will he be all right?'

Kate crossed her fingers superstitiously behind her back, and said, in her most definite voice, 'Yes, he will.'

Then Grant was there, the child in his arms.

'This is Robbie,' he announced, smiling broadly at Kate. 'He actually told me his name.'

Kate sighed her relief. Robbie must have remembered his name as he'd regained consciousness, which was an excellent sign. She tried not to think of Gareth, now convalescing at his home, and crossed her fingers again.

'It doesn't work, crossing fingers,' Grant said, taking her hand and uncrossing them, then lifting the imprisoned hand to his lips and dropping a kiss on the palm. 'What does work is medical knowledge most times, and love and faith at others.'

He paused then added, 'And when those don't suffice, it isn't because we didn't know enough, or do enough, or care enough, but because there's some grand plan that we don't understand, which decrees a person's time has come.'

Kate was so startled by his words she gaped at him. This

hardly sounded like the man so shattered by the death of his baby son he was about to dedicate his life to knowing more about what had killed him.

'You don't mean that,' she said, bending to help the ambulance officer strap young Robbie gently onto the stretcher and roll it into position beside the one on which his sister lay. The children's mother climbed in beside them, and the ambulance officer shut the door.

'I didn't for a long time,' Grant said, his voice quietly convincing, 'but I do now. Lifting this Robbie out, seeing him open his eyes, I remembered the good things about my Robbie, and thought of him without the depth of pain I hadn't, until now, been able to avoid.'

Kate felt as if her heart might break—but whether with sorrow for the love she had for him but could never reveal to him or with happiness that he was started on a real path to recovery, she couldn't tell.

She looked around, seeking some distraction, then realised the other children had already been transported, either home or to the hospital, where they'd be kept until checked again by either her or Grant.

'We have to get back,' she said, pretending she'd been thinking about work all along. 'There'll be a queue at the hospital and a lot of edgy patients in the surgery.'

Grant glanced her way but said nothing, merely collecting her bag and following her towards the car.

But as they drove home, quietly discussing the various theories the rescuers had offered about the cause of the accident, they passed the place where the emu had run into them and saw the fallen body with its long frilled feathers lying beside the road. And beside it, another emu, peering down at the lifeless form, poking at it with its beak.

Once again, Kate felt her heart swell with sadness, and this time she didn't try to stem it, letting it wash over her as if empathy with the big bird might relieve some of her own pain.

'It must have been its mate,' she murmured, the words catching in her throat, coming out far too huskily. 'Emus mate for life. Did you know that?'

She glanced at Grant, but he was looking fixedly ahead, as if piloting her car back to town took all his concentration.

CHAPTER ELEVEN

GRANT went to the hospital while Kate, knowing the badly injured victims had been taken straight to Craigtown, checked with Tara that the baby was still sleeping, with Mr McConagle that he had everything he needed, then headed for the surgery to tackle the backlog of patients.

Having heard about the accident, those waiting were understanding but anxious to hear details and reports on young friends, so every consultation seemed to take for ever. Stopping to feed Cassie put her further behind. Eventually Grant arrived and, using the treatment room for consultations, helped her through the session.

Kate thanked Vi, but as she carried the baby back to the house she felt the emptiness of deep disappointment.

Was it simply that she'd wanted to talk over the accident with him—to talk it out of her system—or was she missing him already, knowing he'd soon be gone? She phoned the hospital and found all but one of the children seen there had been discharged and the one remaining was asleep, his mother by his side. Still edgy, she phoned Craigtown hospital, where medical staff assured her that the bus driver and three children were all resting comfortably.

'And you're not much company,' she told the sleeping Cassie. 'It's night-time feeds you're supposed to sleep through now you're getting older. Not the daytime ones.'

She slouched about the house, getting in Mr McConagle's way until he started to dismantle a wall and shooed her off, telling her to take the baby out for a walk until he was finished making a mess. Maybe a walk wasn't such a bad idea, she decided, lifting Cassie into her stroller and slapping a wide-brimmed hat on her own head. She'd get paint for the walls of the small bedroom. After all, Grant had said he'd help her paint it, though she could hardly paint it while he was sleeping in it, paint fumes being what they were. She'd have to wait till he was gone.

The brightness of the day failed to lift the weight of depression that settled more firmly on her shoulders with this thought, but then her daughter, waking to smile at her as they walked towards the town, reminded her of why she'd shifted to Testament and of the commitment she'd made when Cassie had been little more than a fist-sized foetus.

'We *will* be happy here,' she promised the wide-eyed baby. 'And you and I will make a wonderful life together. For a start, we'll buy some Christmas decorations, things we can keep from year to year, making a tradition for our little family. We'll get a special tree that can be packed away and little ornaments to hang on it, and bright tinsel for the walls. Or is tinsel tacky?'

'I don't think so.'

Grant's voice startled her out of her determinedly cheerful conversation. He'd emerged, again, from Codger Williams's bakery.

Confused by the rush of physical sensation his appearance had caused, Kate took refuge in business, looking pointedly at her watch before saying in a remarkably controlled voice, considering how edgy she was feeling, 'I thought you'd be back at the surgery by now.'

Grant's smile, which had, understandably, been missing all day, twitched about his lips, but all he said was, 'I've five minutes before I'm due to start. I think I'll make it back by then.'

And with that he was gone, striding away, leaving Kate with the lost sensation she'd felt on returning home to find him gone.

'He'll be gone for good before long,' she reminded herself, 'so you'd better get used to it.'

She pushed on resolutely towards the shops, focussing her mind on Christmas decorations, wondering how one cooked a turkey—were they much more complicated than chickens?

Which reminded her of the emu and she sighed.

'You know, Cass,' she said softly to the baby, pausing in the shade of a peppercorn tree to adjust the stroller so the sun didn't strike the chubby limbs, 'I think I might be like the emu. I'm beginning to think things didn't work out with Mark because he wasn't my mate for life, and deep down I knew it. Though, if I'd never met Grant again...'

She couldn't go on, knowing with a deep conviction that infiltrated every cell in her body that *he* was her mate for life.

And he belonged to someone else.

'I guess that happens to hundreds of thousands of people,' she told Cassie, although the baby had drifted back to sleep and probably hadn't been following the conversation too well. 'They don't meet that one person or, if they do, it's the wrong time or place or circumstances.'

On that gloomy note, she pushed the stroller into the newsagent's and with a total lack of excitement or enthusiasm surveyed the array of Christmas decorations the shop had on display.

'I need a tree, and things to go on it, things that will last but nothing poisonous if the baby sucks it, and probably nothing too fragile that will break if she clutches at it, and some tinselly stuff—though she might eat that, mightn't she...?'

Young Jill Ellis, who'd come to serve her, frowned at these requests.

'Won't Grant Bell still be working for you over Christmas?'

'Yes, he's here till the New Year,' Kate replied, annoyed with the young woman for offering a reminder she didn't need. 'What's that got to do with anything?'

'Well, he's just bought a whole heap of Christmas decorations, including our top-of-the-range tree. He asked Dad to deliver them to your place and we guessed he was helping you set up.'

Jill hesitated, then lifted her fingers to her lips as if to take back the words, adding, 'Gosh, it was probably a surprise for you, and I've gone and put my foot in it. But it seemed silly, both of you buying trees.'

'Yes!' Kate said, then she wheeled the stroller around, ready to march out of the shop and back down the street to the surgery, where she'd demand to know what Grant Bell thought he was doing—buying *her* Christmas decorations. Unfortunately, the stroller wheel caught a turntable displaying Christmas cards and the flimsy structure toppled, spreading cards in all directions.

Cassie, jolted awake, began to cry, and by the time Kate had comforted her and helped Jill collect the cards, much of her anger had faded.

Though Grant still had a cheek!

The morning's accident meant some patients had switched from the morning to the afternoon surgery session, so it was late by the time Grant crossed the garden and pushed through the back door of the house.

The house was quiet and he found Katie sitting on the lounge, an assortment of boxes and plastic bags in front of her. As she heard him come in, she turned, then shook her head.

'I went up to buy them and Jill told me you'd already done it.'

Her words were so bleak he hurried over to her, squatting in front of her and taking her hands in his.

'I'm sorry if I spoiled your fun,' he said, massaging her cold fingers, 'but I was up there and I couldn't resist.'

She shrugged as if it didn't matter, confirming this when

she said, 'I don't think I'd have found it as much fun as confusing.'

'So what else is wrong?' he asked, resting his free hand against her cheek.

Another shrug.

'Nothing. Everything.'

She twisted her head away and removed her fingers from his other hand.

'I suppose you know about cooking turkeys as well.'

'Of course, *and* I've ordered one,' he said, standing up and dropping a kiss lightly on the top of her head. What he really wanted to do was take her in his arms and hold her close and promise her everything would be all right, but he wasn't certain that it would be. Not yet. 'So stop fretting about Christmas, and don't start on that perfect mother thing again because Cassie needs love, not perfection, and you've got love by the bucketload, Katie Fenton.'

She looked up at him as she spoke, and the confusion in her eyes proved too much for him. He took her hands in his, drew her to her feet and wrapped his arms around her body, drawing it in to feed warmth into it from his own.

'You're the most generous, sharing, caring person I know,' he said, murmuring the words into her ear. 'And Cassie is the luckiest girl in the world to have you for a mother.'

He tilted up her head and looked deep into her eyes.

'Believe me?'

She shook her head.

'No, but it made me feel better.'

Then she pushed away from him, but not before he saw the sadness still lingering in her lovely eyes.

Grant grabbed her hands and drew her close again.

'I love you, Katie Fenton,' he said quietly. 'Can you hold that thought until I come back?'

She spun away again, glaring now, obviously unaffected by his declaration.

'Come back from where?' she demanded.

'Sydney,' he said, grinning at her wrath. 'Well, Brisbane first and then Sydney. You did say I could have the weekend off, didn't you? And Dr Darling's visiting some old friends and has agreed to fill in for me for the morning sessions tomorrow and Friday. Codger's giving me a lift to Craigtown in the morning and I'll fly to Brisbane, then go on to Sydney Friday afternoon. I'll be back Monday afternoon so, if you could get Tara to mind Cassie and do that morning session, I'll do the evening.'

He paused, then couldn't resist adding, 'I do hope it doesn't interfere with your date with Brian.'

'It's not a date and don't tell me how to organise my practice,' Kate snapped at him, hurrying into the kitchen before his too-perceptive eyes saw her despair. 'How did you know about Dr Darling? And is he qualified to practise still? He's got to be about a hundred.'

Kate knew her anger was misdirected, but she had to release it or go mad, so she fumed on, blaming Vi, blaming anyone, when all along her heart was breaking because she knew exactly why Grant was going back to Sydney. He was going to see Linda.

He might love Katie Fenton—as a friend he'd known for a long time—but Linda was his lover, his fiancée...

His mate for life?

The thought hurt so much she had to close her eyes for a moment, willing tears she no longer shed so freely to remain at bay and the painful thudding in her chest to subside.

With hands that barely trembled, she peeled vegetables for their dinner, put lamb chops under the grill, even made a salad.

You knew all along he'd be going, she kept telling herself, but the desolation in her heart, over his departure for just a few days, suggested she'd been subconsciously harbouring the most ridiculous hopes and dreams.

Somehow they got through the meal, conversation about patients covering an underlying tension so brittle Kate wondered their words didn't crackle in the air. Grant excused himself to pack—she wanted to ask how long it took to pack four Hawaiian shirts and three pairs of board shorts—and she washed the dishes, then willed Cassie to wake up so she'd have an excuse to disappear into her bedroom.

He was gone by the time Kate got up in the morning, leaving a note with his mother's address and phone number in Sydney 'in case you need to contact me about a patient or if there's anything you'd like me to pick up in the city.'

Angry and frustrated because she knew she had no right to be, Kate tore the note up, then had to retrieve all the pieces with the number and sticky tape them together in case she *did* need to contact him about a patient.

Mr McConagle arrived and because it was going to be a sawdusty day, she packed up what Cassie would need and took her down the road to Tara's.

'I'll just see Dr Darling has all he needs, then be back to feed her,' she explained to Tara. 'Then I suppose I could take her for a walk uptown. Honestly! I'd have been better off doing all the surgery sessions myself. I don't know why Grant got Dr Darling to come in.'

'Because the old fellow loves to keep his hand in,' Tara's mother told her, 'and the folk in town who knew him love to see him again. He's always done a few sessions when he's been visiting.'

Kate left their house, grumpier than ever. Why hadn't she known that?

And if Dr Darling liked to do a bit of locum work, why hadn't Vi contacted him instead of Grant?

The puzzle prodded her into asking Vi, who merely smiled at her, shrugged her shoulders, then said, 'Grant was available and, though you mightn't realise it, he needed help as much as you did, Kate. Needed to get away from the city for a while as well.'

Kate was about to point out that he *had* been away from the city at the time, but Dr Darling arrived at that moment, greeting her with a warm hug and assurances that he could still remember most of the medicine he'd learnt.

'I've got old, Katie, not stupid,' he said, smiling delightedly at her. 'Now, where's this baby of yours? When am I going to meet her?'

He was so like the kind and loving man she remembered that her bad mood subsided and she found herself inviting him to come to lunch—to see the house and what she was doing to it and to meet Cassie.

Collecting Cassie from Tara, she returned home, tidied up and prepared salads for their lunch, trying desperately to keep her mind off planes winging towards the city and a certain passenger on a certain plane...

The day dragged slowly by. She phoned Brian. He'd been so hurt when she'd turned down his offer of a loan and had accepted the bank loan instead that she hadn't liked to cry off the dinner-dance. But now she did, using Grant's absence as an excuse to avoid the Christmas party, but in her heart knowing Grant had been right—it would have been a date, and to go on a date with Brian, now she realised how she felt about another man, would have been unfair.

The weekend brought its usual spate of minor accidents, and the casualties coming into the hospital kept her busier than usual. So much so that as she sank, exhausted, into bed on Sunday evening, she reminded herself to contact the Health Department. If they didn't have a doctor starting at the hospital in the New Year, she'd have to rev up the board and community and organise protests and petitions to the local members of parliament.

At least, she thought, smiling wryly into the darkness, it

would keep her mind off Grant's departure, and the heartbreak and loneliness she knew would follow it.

On Monday morning, she left Cassie at Tara's place again so Mr McConagle could hammer and saw without thought for the baby, and as she walked back to start surgery she looked around her, recalling the joy she'd felt as she'd walked these streets when she'd first returned, remembering the certainty that had told her she'd done the right thing.

Now Christmas decorations flapped on telegraph poles and Christmas lights were strung across the street, and though she knew that every day she spent with Grant would make his final departure that much harder, at least she'd have his company for Christmas and memories of that special day to hold in her heart for ever.

Morning surgery seemed to go on endlessly, and by the time it finished she was so anxious about Grant's return she collected Cassie from Tara and walked up to the bakery, casually asking Codger, as she bought a loaf of raisin bread, if he was picking up his friend from Craigtown.

Codger looked startled, then shook his head.

'Hell, I hope not! I'm sure he didn't mention it—and if he did, I've forgotten. The Monday flight comes in at about eleven.'

He frowned at Kate, then added, 'Actually, I was under the impression he was driving back.'

More confused than ever, she walked home, realised Mr McConagle was still hammering and, after a quick lunch, sought refuge in the surgery, Cassie sleeping in her basket there while Kate caught up on some paperwork.

So when the strange car pulled into her drive, she had a good view of it—and a vague impression of someone in the passenger seat. She moved to the window to get a better view. Grant was driving and there was definitely a woman sitting beside him.

He'd brought Linda back with him!

Kate's heart faltered so badly she had to put a hand against the wall to steady herself. Of course he'd want to spend Christmas with his fiancée, she told herself, but the aching emptiness of unacknowledged love drained all the energy from her body and left her so weak she wondered how she'd get through the rest of the day, let alone another fortnight of Grant's presence in the town.

Then she steadied herself and straightened up, stiffening her spine and tilting her chin. For a start, he could shift to Vi's. She'd tell him she needed to decorate the small bedroom for the baby.

Then she needn't see him at all. He'd do some sessions, she'd do others, and their paths needn't cross.

But he was going to cook the turkey, an inner voice wailed. And you were waiting until he returned to put up the decorations.

'He can damn well take them to Vi's as well,' Kate muttered to herself, then she leaned closer to the window, realising for the first time that he had a trailer hooked on behind the car. A loaded trailer covered by a grey tarpaulin.

Maybe it was another motorbike—maybe Linda rode one as well.

A light tap on the door, then Grant was there, opening his arms to her as he had on the day he'd first arrived.

'I'm back,' he said, smiling so broadly he seemed to shine with an inner radiance.

'So I can see,' Kate said crisply, determined not to let the radiance thing get to her—or to reveal her own devastation.

'Well, aren't you going to kiss me?' he asked, holding out his arms again.

'Why the hell should I kiss you?' Kate demanded. 'You're my locum, not my lover.'

And though he should have been put firmly in his place by that pronouncement, the wretch continued to smile, and the twinkle in his eyes positively gleamed with delight.

'Ah, but we were, and could have been again, remember.'

'That was different,' Kate muttered, aware the heat burning inside her must have washed colour into her cheeks.

'Was it, Katie?' he said softly, moving closer. 'Oh, I know you said it was just comfort you were offering, but it seemed very much like love to me. Isn't comfort an element of love?'

'I don't know what you're talking about, and even if I did I wouldn't listen,' Kate snapped, as angry with the foolish hope that had risen in her heart as she was with this two-timing male in front of her. 'I don't know how you can talk that way, with Linda outside in my garden.'

'Linda in your garden?' Grant looked genuinely confused, then his face cleared and he laughed with such delight Kate wanted to hit him. 'That's not Linda, that's Mum. Actually, Linda doesn't exist—never did—and I thought Cassie needed a grandmother so I brought Mum back to get started with that side of things. She'll stay with Vi, of course, but mind Cassie for you—for us—whenever we can't get Tara.'

Kate shook her head. This was a worse conversation than they'd had the day he'd ridden into Testament four weeks ago. But there was so much she didn't understand that she didn't know where to start. With 'Linda doesn't exist'? Heavens! Her heart was cavorting so madly she was afraid she might have misheard him, in which case she'd better not ask...

Then there was the 'us' thing he was going on about...

She was still hesitating when he took the last step needed to bring him into touching distance, so her physical reaction caused further chaos in her mind.

'Kiss me, Katie,' he murmured. 'Kiss me then tell me there's no us!'

The last working cell in her brain registered that he'd often seemed to know exactly what she'd been thinking, then she gave in to the hands drawing her closer and lifted her face towards his, accepting his kiss and kissing him back.

Then she remembered Linda, and pushed away.

'What did you mean—Linda doesn't exist?' she demanded, hope battling with apprehension—but she had to know.

'I made her up,' Grant told her, his smile so broad she knew he thought this had been sheer brilliance, though all it was to her was unbelievable.

'Made up a fiancée? Why on earth would you do that?'

'So you'd feel safe with me, not feel threatened having a man about the house—you know, after Mark...'

Kate didn't know, but her body, still close enough to Grant's to feel his warmth, seemed delighted to learn that Linda was pure fiction.

Though when she considered the anguish this fictional woman had caused her...

She was about to give voice to her disapproval of this tactic when Grant drew her close again, and this second kiss blanked out her mind completely, leaving room only for emotion and the physical responses as old as time itself.

Grant felt the passion in her response, and the final coil of terrible tension he seemed to have carried for so long unwound from his body.

'I love you, Katie,' he said, drawing her close against him and burying his head in her fragrant, tangled hair. 'I think I realised that soon after I came back, but I wasn't over Robbie's death—couldn't handle commitment that included another baby—so I tried to ignore it. I told myself specialty training was more important anyway—that what I'd learn or might discover could benefit so many babies in the future. But when I lifted the other Robbie out of that bus, I knew that you do what you can in this life, and contributing happiness, any time or any place, is just as important as contributing to great scientific discoveries.'

He felt the woman in his arms move and added, 'Well, maybe not quite as important, but I was an average student at best, and a man or woman twice as bright as me will now have the opportunity to do the work I thought I wanted to do.'

This time the movement was more definite—in fact, the woman to whom he was so ardently professing his love was actually pushing him away from her. He looked down and saw the fire flashing in her green eyes.

'Are you telling me you've given up the speciality training?'

Uncertain what was angering her, and knowing it was best to tread warily with his Katie in this mood, Grant nodded.

'To do what?' she demanded, her eyes narrowing dangerously.

He grinned, couldn't help it, and held out his arms again.

'To be the hospital doctor at Testament. Though, actually, when I talked to the Health Department people, I did mention they might be able to restructure the position so I've rights of private practice and we can sort of run the hospital and surgery jointly—the two of us, you know...'

His voice tailed off as he realised she looked, if anything, even fiercer.

'And you didn't think to mention any of this to me? You say you love me then rearrange both our futures without any consultation whatsoever? How do you think I feel, having you sacrifice your dream of paediatric oncology for me? What kind of burden is that for me to carry?'

'Ah!' Grant murmured, and drew her close again. 'So that's what's got you fired up!' He tilted up her chin so their eyes met. 'It was no dream, no sacrifice, Katie. When Robbie was born I set aside my first dream, to have a property again, replacing it with the wonderful vision of fatherhood. Then, when he died, that dream died with him. I went in the direction of paediatric oncology because I was so lost I didn't know what else to do, and I knew that drifting aimlessly would lead to disaster.'

He saw a softening in her eyes and knew she understood, and when she murmured 'And then?' he continued, confident now that he'd found his way again.

'I came back to Testament, and remembered all I'd loved about life in the country. I felt at home again, and more at peace than I'd been for a long time. You were part of that healing—seeing you again, being with you, feeling that intensity that had been missing from my life for so long.'

'But you still didn't share any of this with me,' she protested, but so weakly he knew it was a token argument.

'I wanted to make sure I *could* come back—that I could get out of my commitment in Sydney without leaving the department short-staffed. I also needed to know if I could get a job out here. I spoke to officials over the phone, but had to be interviewed in Brisbane. I didn't want to get your hopes up then let you down—but if it hadn't been now, it would have been soon that I'd have come back because, having found you again, my mate for life, I was darned if I was going to lose you.'

Kate was so overwhelmed by all this information she forgot the other questions and objections she might have made, and when he leaned forward to kiss her again, she gave herself up to the delight of being in his arms, and with all her heart and soul returned the kiss.

The sound of Cassie's waking cry broke them apart and, though Kate moved towards the door, it was Grant who got there first, picking up the baby girl and cradling her in his arms, his face glowing with the love he was now unafraid to show.

'I'd better introduce her to Mum, then get the trailer unpacked. We can leave the furniture in the garage until we get Cassie's room painted. I'll start on it this week.'

Kate, still bemused by the rapidity of the changes taking place in her life, followed him out of the surgery. She'd been about to ask, And where are you going to sleep? when a tide of heat rushed through her. She knew exactly where Grant was going to sleep. Not only tonight, but every night for a very long time.

By Christmas Eve the new bathroom was finished and the altered guest bedroom restored to its original purpose. Cassie's room was not only painted and decorated, but furnished with white baby furniture, brightened by small decals of ducks and ducklings—the precious furniture Grant had brought with him on the trailer.

Grant and Katie stood beside the crib, looking down at the sleeping infant.

'I want to adopt her, you know,' Grant said, 'so she's officially mine as well as just belonging to me.'

Katie felt her heart swell with so much love she wondered it could all be contained within the confines of so small a part of her—then she remembered how Grant's love seemed to permeate all of her, not just her heart.

Permeated the whole house, so it was in the air she breathed, the food she ate.

'Don't you want me to?' he asked, shocking her out of her fantasy.

'Of course,' she said, turning to look at him so he'd know she meant what she was saying. 'It's just that you continue to surprise me—to overwhelm me—with your love. You take my breath away.'

'I know other ways I can do that,' he suggested, and Kate knew, from his smile and the light in his brilliant blue eyes, that her love for him had also worked some magic. Grant had come as her knight in shining armour, charging to the rescue of the maiden in distress, but together they'd vanquished the dragons of the past, and she and Cassie had brought him safely home.

Modern Romance™
...seduction and
passion guaranteed

Tender Romance™
...love affairs that
last a lifetime

Sensual Romance™
...sassy, sexy and
seductive

Blaze
...sultry days and
steamy nights

Medical Romance™
...medical drama on
the pulse

Historical Romance™
...rich, vivid and
passionate

27 new titles every month.

*With all kinds of Romance for
every kind of mood...*

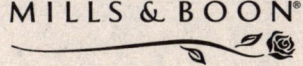

MILLS & BOON

Medical Romance™

ASSIGNMENT: SINGLE FATHER
by Caroline Anderson

Working as a practice nurse in Dr Xavier Giraud's surgery and caring for his children had seemed perfect for Fran after the traumas of A&E. Except she fell in love with him and he could never submit to his love for her in return. Where could her relationship with Xavier go? She was compelled to stay and find out...

MORE THAN A GIFT *by Josie Metcalfe*

After waiting for ever for love, Laurel was devastated when she had to leave consultant Dmitri Rostropovich behind. Now, eight months pregnant and trapped in a snowbound car, she can only wonder if she will ever see him again. Dmitri is searching for her. He's close – very close – but will he find her in time...?

DR BLAKE'S ANGEL *by Marion Lennox*

Dr Blake Sutherland was the sole GP in town – overworked and exhausted, he needed a miracle. He got one in the form of pregnant Dr Nell McKenzie, who insisted she took over his practice! He couldn't possibly let her, so they agreed to share his patients – and Christmas. Blake had a feeling this Christmas would be one he'd never forget...

On sale 6th December 2002

Available at most branches of WH Smith, Tesco, Martins, Borders, Eason, Sainsbury's and all good paperback bookshops.

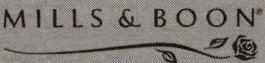

Medical Romance™

HOME BY CHRISTMAS *by Jennifer Taylor*

Christmas in the children's intensive care unit is always an emotional time, and especially so this year. Dr Lisa Bennett has until Christmas to decide whether to accept another man's proposal, and consultant surgeon Will Saunders has until Christmas Eve to help her realise that the life she should be daring to share – is his!

EMERGENCY: CHRISTMAS *by Alison Roberts*

Penny only started dating Dr Mark Wallace to make another man jealous – then discovered she'd done the right thing by accident! Their Christmas wedding would be perfect... But now the past was threatening to destroy their love – and a terrifying attack in the emergency room might mean they'd never get a second chance...

CHRISTMAS IN PARIS *by Margaret Barker*

When Dr Alyssa Ferguson returned to work in her beloved Paris, the last person she expected to see was her ex-lover, Pierre Dupont – and now he was her boss! As they began to rekindle their passionate romance, Pierre made Alyssa realise she had to face up to the past. Maybe they could look forward to a blissful Christmas in Paris together...

On sale 6th December 2002

Available at most branches of WH Smith, Tesco, Martins, Borders, Eason, Sainsbury's and all good paperback bookshops.

Double Destiny

There is more than one route to happiness.

Mills & Boon® Tender Romance™ and Medical Romance™ present a gripping, emotional two-part series from leading author **Caroline Anderson**.

Destiny has more than one plan for Fran Williams — it has two: rich, wealthy and energetic Josh Nicholson and charming, sensual, single father Dr Xavier Giraud!

Can a woman choose her own destiny? Could there be more than one Mr Right?

Follow Fran's parallel destinies in:

<u>November 2002</u>
ASSIGNMENT: SINGLE MAN
in Tender Romance™

<u>December 2002</u>
ASSIGNMENT: SINGLE FATHER
in Medical Romance™

Plus *read about Fran's first fateful meetings with Josh Nicholson and Xavier Giraud — for free. Look for DOUBLE DESTINY at www.millsandboon.co.uk*

Don't miss *Book Four* of this BRAND-NEW 12 book collection 'Bachelor Auction'.

Who says money can't buy love?

On sale 6th December

Available at most branches of WH Smith, Tesco, Martins, Borders, Eason, Sainsbury's, and all good paperback bookshops.

BA/RTL/4

2 Books
and a surprise gift!

We would like to take this opportunity to thank you for reading this Mills & Boon® book by offering you the chance to take TWO more specially selected titles from the Medical Romance™ series absolutely FREE! We're also making this offer to introduce you to the benefits of the Reader Service™—

- ★ FREE home delivery
- ★ FREE gifts and competitions
- ★ FREE monthly Newsletter
- ★ Books available before they're in the shops
- ★ Exclusive Reader Service discount

Accepting these FREE books and gift places you under no obligation to buy; you may cancel at any time, even after receiving your free shipment. Simply complete your details below and return the entire page to the address below. ***You don't even need a stamp!***

YES! Please send me 2 free Medical Romance books and a surprise gift. I understand that unless you hear from me, I will receive 4 superb new titles every month for just £2.55 each, postage and packing free. I am under no obligation to purchase any books and may cancel my subscription at any time. The free books and gift will be mine to keep in any case.

M2ZEB

Ms/Mrs/Miss/Mr ....Initials............................
BLOCK CAPITALS PLEASE

Surname..

Address...

....

....Postcode ....

Send this whole page to:
UK: The Reader Service, FREEPOST CN81, Croydon, CR9 3WZ
EIRE: The Reader Service, PO Box 4546, Kilcock, County Kildare (stamp required)

Offer not valid to current Reader Service subscribers to this series. We reserve the right to refuse an application and applicants must be aged 18 years or over. Only one application per household. Terms and prices subject to change without notice. Offer expires 28th February 2003. As a result of this application, you may receive offers from Harlequin Mills & Boon and other carefully selected companies. If you would prefer not to share in this opportunity please write to The Data Manager at the address above.

Mills & Boon® is a registered trademark owned by Harlequin Mills & Boon Limited.
Medical Romance ™ is being used as a trademark.